Hoarfrost

and

Cherry Blossoms

Susan Bainbridge

Strategic Book Group

Strategic Book Group
P.O. Box 333
Durham CT 06422
www.StrategicBookClub.com

ISBN 978-1-60976-590-3

Printed in the United States of America

Book Design/Layout by: Andrew Herzog

Dedication

To Brian, my catalyst

To my sister Cindy and my good friend Carol,
the hot air in my balloon

To my children, Matthew, Melissa and Robert,
for appreciating the random and the ridiculous.

To my Father Bob (Speed) and to my late
Mother Joan for . . . well . . . everything!

I

The Last Trupper

Chapter One

$\mathcal{I}$t was funny. It really was funny. He was dead. That actually wasn't funny. But we all die eventually. We can only hope to die in some interesting way; some memorable scene that makes for a good story for years to come. That's what Brian had always envisioned, a really extraordinary death; something that would keep people talking for generations. So when he and Mary found old Johnny Michael, in his navy work parka, wolverine fur framing his tanned, leathered face, sitting against that tree, frozen solid, his first reaction was actually jealousy. What a great way to go! Years from now, someone would be saying, "Yes, my grandfather froze to death in the Arctic. He sat down, back up against a tree, legs stretched straight out and crossed, arms folded across his chest. Not huddled up in the foetal position whimpering, no not him. Defiant and confident to the end, that was Granddad." Brian didn't see the levity in it, not yet, that would come later as events unfolded.

"What are we going to do? We're in the middle of nowhere." Mary was pacing in a small circle. She did this whenever she was upset.

Brian raised his eyebrows, took his hands out of his massive, moose-hide mittens and rubbed his mouth. "Better us than the wolves next spring."

"Oh my God, shut up!" Mary plopped down in the snow and stared at Johnny. Brian sat down beside her and set his gaze on the frozen spectacle. It was 1975, long before digital cameras and cell phones, so the scene could only be recorded to memory. They sat in silence digesting the situation. They had found a neighbour who had died on the job. No foul play, no mysterious circumstances, just the end of one man's life.

Johnny had been a trapper for as long as anyone could remember. He worked his line regularly and would be gone for five to six weeks at a time. There were stories that he had come north as a prospector; made enough money to retire, but as so many blinded by gold fever do, had blown it in a matter of a few years on outrageous purchases.

Brian's favourite Johnny tale was the corn flakes saga. Apparently, he was sitting in a bar in Edmonton one summer talking with some locals about the Arctic winter. He was trying to describe snowshoeing to them. Snowshoes were used to walk on top of the snow and Indians had developed different shapes and sizes depending on the snow with which they had to deal. In the east they were often called 'bear paws' because they were only about three feet long but almost three feet wide. It was impossible to stand with your feet together without dislocating your groin, so there was a clever gait you developed which never saw both shoes touch the snow at the same time. In the far northwest the snow was drier and flaked in thin layers. This Arctic snowshoe was made the same way, with wet wood bent into a teardrop shape and then animal sinew, the tendon that holds muscles to bones, woven in a special pattern across the wooden frame. But the shape was different. The shoes were much longer and narrower. Johnny was trying to explain to the locals the special gait required for these Arctic shoes. They were all standing up trying to copy his rhythm. But it was hard to get the feel of it on the hardwood floor. Johnny was frustrated and more than a little drunk and he wanted to give these guys a real lesson in Arctic trekking, so he ordered in corn flakes . . . truckloads of corn flakes. It took seven hours to fill the bar with enough cereal to replicate an Arctic trail. The lessons went on for a couple of days, people coming in for a pint and a snowshoe lesson. That's how you blow a retirement fund in a couple of years!

They say that everyone in the north is running or hiding from someone or something. Johnny was no different. He kept to himself and apparently there was an ex-wife and children somewhere, but no evidence of it. Not many wives would have been impressed with the corn flakes scenario. A Mrs. Michael would have preferred corn flakes on the breakfast table, not on a bar room floor.

That's what Brian was thinking about as they sat and stared at Johnny, corn flakes. He tried to think of other aspects of Johnny's life, but his mind was fixated on an Edmonton bar piled high with cereal. He tried looking away, and scanning the snow-capped spruce trees surrounding them, but each time his eyes came back to rest on the frozen corpse, the corn flake images returned. He sighed deeply as he turned his head and stared off into the white canopy that enveloped the forest.

"I've never seen a dead body outside of a funeral home before," Mary whispered as she slipped her hand through Brian's arm. "This may sound stupid, but he looks far more beautiful than anyone I've ever seen lying in a coffin."

"That's probably one of the reasons he came north. So he'd never be confined to a damn coffin. Gladiolas and prayer books and some minister you only met once talking about what a fine man you were, celebrating your life with quotes that no one can understand. It's all bull shit. This is the way a man should die, with a buddy sitting close by, thinking about corn flakes."

Mary tilted her head at Brian, more than a little confused. What the hell was he talking about now? She was often mystified by Brian's comments. Many times his mind would venture off in

strange directions and she regularly found herself
trying to interpret his thoughts.

The north is a haven for the loner—the alpha
male who cannot be confined to the dens created in towns and cities. Some arrive to look for
gold. Others drive up in the summer to check it
out, have car trouble and never leave. The small
towns in the north are full of people still waiting for parts for their cars to arrive. Almost every
house has an old beater parked out front waiting for that alternator or piston. The rusted old
wrecks are like some kind of weird insurance
policy in case they change their mind and want
to head south again.

Along with the old, dead vehicles comes a
type of person whose eyes brim with defiance.
Mary had always been fascinated by Johnny's
deep, penetrating eyes. The north attracted per-
sonalities that shone through such eyes, intelligent and creative people who, for various reasons, chose not to deal with mainstream society.
Renegades attracted to the last frontier, a place
where they could be themselves, and live and die
on their own terms.

Brian was trying to think through the prac-
ticalities of the current dilemma. What exactly
should they do with Johnny? No one would
know for hours that they had even found him.
First Brian and Mary would have to trek back
out the two kilometres to the road and find the
Mounties. Well, the Mountie. Jackson Pedley
was the only Royal Canadian Mounted Police in

the area. Theirs was a one-cop town and quite honestly he was not very busy. Johnny Michael's death would be the highlight of the winter and it was pretty obvious that there was no foul play, just nature once again securing her position as the dominant force.

Mary and Brian had been out trying to stake a claim. Things had not been going very well. The four-inch by four-inch six-foot timber was green and weighed a ton! They needed four of them, one for each corner of the section of land they wanted to register. The plastic toboggan had been a bad idea. The stakes had continually slid off the smooth surface every few feet and they had been cursing the stakes, the toboggan, the snow, the cold and finally each other for the past hour.

The idea of staking a claim had sounded really good last night at the bar. After all, how many people actually lived in the Yukon? It was a unique chance to bring back a great souvenir. Stake your own claim, register the papers, get a topographical map of the area and have the mining agent mark and stamp your claim on it. Mary could see it beautifully framed and hanging in her living room. "Yes, that's the claim I staked, while I was living north of sixty." The sixtieth parallel north is the border for northern Canada, so the Arctic is often referred to as 'north of sixty'.

They never imagined that they would be dumping the stakes and tying Johnny Michael, on his back, legs crossed and sticking straight up perpendicular to the sled, and pulling him back out to the Alaskan Highway. But that was Brian's plan. After all, it wasn't as if they could call an ambulance and it seemed wrong to leave Johnny alone in the wilderness.

The plastic toboggan really had been a bad idea! It was apparent from the start that Johnny was not going to stay in place. Brian pulled the sled and Mary had the job of hanging on to his ankles so he would not tilt left or right. Not an easy task since she could not wear her snowshoes and walk close enough to the sled to get a firm grip. No snowshoes were making the trip almost impossible. Every two or three steps one of Mary's legs would suddenly sink down to her crotch in the snow, she would let go of Johnny's ankles which would flop left or right onto the trail, Brian would have to stop and tilt him up while Mary dug herself out of the hole and positioned herself beside Johnny's legs again.

"This isn't working!" Brian told her. "At this rate we'll never make it to the highway by dark. You need to sit on his chest and hold his legs and then I can make good time."

"Are you out of your mind? I can't sit on a corpse!"

"Well what are we going to do? He's sliding off the goddamned sled every two feet!"

"I'll pull the damn thing and YOU sit on him!" shouted Mary.

"You couldn't even pull it with the stakes strapped on! I'm pulling the sled; I'm the man!"

"Oh yeah, and I'm gonna sit on the frozen corpse 'cause I'm the woman! We should have just left him at the tree and gone for Jackson."

"Yeah, but we didn't. Come on Mary…I'll walk as fast as I can. We can be at the truck in less than an hour. It won't be very funny if the sun starts to set!"

"You're a prick, Brian Ladley!"

"Put a snowshoe on his chest and then sit on the shoe. You won't actually be touching his chest," Brian removed his beaver skin hat and wiped the sweat from his forehead.

Mary positioned a snowshoe on Johnny's chest, swung her leg over him, plunked herself down on the frozen form, her butt in Johnny's face and grabbed onto the legs facing her. She turned her head around and hollered at Brian to begin. It actually worked very well and Brian was able to cover ground quickly. The plastic toboggan cooperated a little better with the additional weight on it, but there were still a few slopes which found Mary and Johnny sliding past Brian and pulling him the rest of the way down the hill.

They had only been walking an hour when they had found Johnny sitting against the tree, but it took three hours to reach the road pulling his body back. Brian started the truck and pumped the heat up to high, while Mary sat down on the bank and stared at the road.

The highway was always quiet by late afternoon. The big trucks heading back and forth from the south always travelled early morning until mid-afternoon. This was a treacherous road in any season, but by travelling at the same time of day at least someone would be close by if you needed help. The Alaskan Highway runs from Dawson Creek, British Columbia, to Fairbanks, Alaska. It was built in only eight months by ten thousand U.S. soldiers in 1942 in order to bring military supplies to their troops in Alaska. At a length of 1,522 miles, it was an amazing accomplishment and was North America's first permanent road built through the tundra. By the early 1970s it was still a dirt road, icy and dangerous in winter, dusty or muddy in summer. During the winter there were no gas stations or homes occupied between towns, so you could drive three hundred miles without seeing a thing besides trees and snow, and the odd boarded up summer gas station. So there they sat in the silence, Brian, Mary and Johnny. They had placed Johnny back on his rump so he was at least sitting beside them rather then lying there with his legs sticking straight up in the air. They were sticky and sweaty; he was still frozen hard as a rock.

Bringing him back to town would have been a simple thing if Brian had emptied out the back of his truck the night before. But he had not. It was still full of beer cases from the hotel that he was going to deliver to the gas station for pick up later that day. There were a lot of cases. The guys had placed a sheet of plywood on each side of the truck box to act as walls, and loaded the empty cases four feet high, strapped down neatly and securely.

"I'm not taking all those cases off the truck. It'll mean another trip back out here and this took us an hour to load up last night," said Brian.

"We can't fit him in the cab with his legs out like that, and even if we could, he would thaw out," Mary shivered at the thought.

"Okay then, we sit him on the toboggan, put a rope around his waist, tilt the toboggan on the back bumper, I get on top of the beer and pull him up top. You push on his feet once I start pulling."

The idea worked and within ten minutes Johnny was sitting up top on fifty cases of beer, leaning against the cab's back window, legs crossed and strapped in securely, and facing south. In a sense, it seemed symbolic; his final farewell to the land that had driven him north in the first place.

Brian and Mary jumped into the warm cab and began the drive into town. Mary's mind wandered off to *The Cremation of Sam McGee*, a poem she had been reading with her students. "I guess this is nothing Robert Service hadn't already heard about. I wonder how many other people have found frozen friends in this cold and isolated corner of the world."

"There are strange things done 'neath the midnight sun

By the men who moil for gold.
The arctic trails have their secret tales
That would make your blood run cold."

Mary leaned her head against the truck window and stared out at the vast, white landscape. This massive, freezing country never left you bored. That's for sure. Always some weird or random thing happening.

Chapter Two

Northern towns are pretty self-sufficient when they can operate on a primitive level. The people become survival savvy quickly. When it's a matter of life or death, it's amazing how much information a person can retain and categorize for later use. Kerosene lamps, wood fires, a log cabin and dry food can keep a person nice and comfortable through a six-month winter.

It is only when the comforts of the south are added to the equation that life can become complicated. Electricity is a wonderful thing, until it goes off at three in the morning and the temperature is minus 40 degrees Fahrenheit outside. Fresh fruit and vegetables are marvellous also, until a glacier blocks the road and it takes the MOT (Ministry of Transport) crews two weeks to open up the highway again.

Most people enjoyed the luxuries of the south, but no one ever quite set up home in a

Toronto fashion. Every kitchen kept some form of wood stove for back up heat. Kerosene lamps were kept handy and everyone had a larder full of canned and dried food, just in case.

As with the rest of the world, garbage was an issue. The territorial government had been quick to begin early recycling programs. Since eighty percent of the glass refuse was beer bottles, it was the first pilot project set in place. This was a good thing. Otherwise astronauts would be able to locate towns north of sixty from space with no problem at all, just by looking for the massive brown, glass pyramids dotting the landscape. There might have actually been some tourist value in the pyramid idea, but it never really caught on. Instead, government trucks made regular runs up and down the highway, picking up empties every couple of days. Like any program with very long-term goals, it does not initially interest the average person, so the Beer Bottle Retrieval Program paid two cents a bottle. This is why Brian's truck was loaded up with cases of beer. He made about twenty-five dollars a load, which paid for his drinking until the next pick up. Actually it paid for more than his consumption, but Brian liked company, and in a bar, that meant picking up the tab regularly.

In this last frontier there were only a handful of residents over forty. Not many people chose to retire in this climate. At thirty, Brian was almost middle-age in northern terms, and good-looking, in an ordinary sort of way. In towns with a population of five hundred to a thousand, every resident is important and feels unique and valuable. Everet was big at nine hundred and fifty souls. Once you accounted for the children, the married folk and single women that left about one hundred single men. So an ordinary looking guy usually turned into something quite special in Everet. Unfortunately, the odds were still on the side of women. The north is a harsh place and not many beautiful young women venture outside comfortable cities and towns.

God has a great sense of humour and enjoys the sitcoms he has created. One popular show is the *Biology of the Tundra*. It's based on the northern terrain and climate and the type of person who chooses to live there. His frontiers naturally attract hardy and healthy young men searching for new territory to mark. It also naturally attracts strong, aggressive women looking for their own corner of the world. Like the testosterone-driven man, this adventuresome woman is also looking for a beautiful young female. So the competition for a ripe, young mate becomes more dynamic and interesting.

Brian did not mind the competition, be it male or female. He felt good for various reasons. He was the third brother in a family of six, and stuck right in the middle. He carried with him classic middle-child baggage, and so the north gave him that feeling of importance he had never received at home. He felt attractive, worthy and since he had latched on to Mary, very cool and sexy.

Mary liked his five-foot ten inch stature and his lean, muscular build. She said that she preferred to look a partner in the eye and thought that he was a perfect height just three inches taller than her. She also liked his chiselled face, which had the potential to turn rather severe as the years passed, but was quite striking now. His eyes were a beautiful emerald green. They were his greatest asset, but he often told her that was only because they were away from home. His whole family had the same eyes, so he was nothing special back on Worthington Street in Winnipeg. But here in Everet they were magnificent eyes. Mary actually got tired of people commenting on them. "Don't Brian's eyes just mesmerize you?" or "I can't stop looking at Brian's eyes!" She usually just agreed and moved on to other topics. She was pretty secure in the relationship, so jealously was not a factor. He was hers, as long as she wanted him and right now that was good enough.

He had a mild cowboy swagger when he walked. Not as extreme as the bow-legged professionals, but very macho nonetheless. Somewhere between Edmonton and Toronto men lose the swagger, and the cowboy hat. Coming from Winnipeg gave him options and he could swing both ways; jump onto a bale of hay at a rodeo or sit at an ethnic café in Toronto and sip on coffee and grappa. Mary liked that about him. He was full of masculine airs, yet he could be dressed up and taken out on vacations. It was a nice combo and Mary often wondered why men from Winnipeg were not more famous. Maybe the Winnipeg women kept them a secret. On the other hand, she thought, they were heard of over the years. During both World Wars, the combat pilots from Winnipeg were infamous. Perhaps it was that magic blend of east and west that created a man with the patience to learn to fly and the balls to fly over Germany. But if you were an eastern girl or a western girl, perhaps you were looking for a thoroughbred.

Brian felt like he had reached his pinnacle. He was feeling handsome, macho and confident. It was that moment in his life where he was well-pleased with everything; his body, his mind and his purpose. He was enjoying his Camelot.

Brian liked Mary's sense of humour. They both enjoyed a good laugh, which meant that they found a joke in almost any situation. There are people who find most situations in life stressful, and spend most of their time 'stressing over the stressfulness' of it all, and then there are those who believe that most disastrous events are out of their hands, and they look for the humour. Both are okay, since each apparently enjoys either the lamenting or the laughing, but perhaps the latter is healthier. Brian and Mary certainly enjoyed the laughing. They laughed together about Mary's abscessed tooth and the drunken dentist who tried to pull it. They laughed about the time that a good friend was out with his buddies the night before his wedding and they had placed him, drunk, on a flight to Edmonton. And they laughed about the time that Brian was sitting in a plane on the tarmac waiting to fly south and the wing of the plane fell off. Just fell off! These were stories that were either disconcerting or very funny depending on your view of life. To that stressed out half of society these would be major annoyances, but to Brian and Mary they were a source of endless amusement and entertainment. They loved a good story! They had no idea that they were in the middle of a new tale that would be told for generations.

They drove into town at dusk. Dusk lasts a long time in the north. That time between night and day can seem endless, depending on the time of year. In the winter, dusk can last for hours. The sun hangs on a distant horizon for most of the day. So at four o'clock in the afternoon, the town of Everet sat dull and dark and cold. The silhouette of Brian's truck cast a long shadow and Johnny's head stretched out across the road.

"Where should we take him?" asked Mary.

"I don't know. Where do you take a frozen trapper sittin' in the back of your truck?"

"On top of a pile of beer cases!" Mary turned to look out the back window at Johnny.

"To the bar!" they both said in unison as they each stretched their arms and pointed in the same direction.

That did not seem like a bad idea, since that was where everyone in town gathered on any given Saturday evening. The Mountie, the mayor or the priest would certainly be there and they needed at least one of them. They were not sure who specialized in this type of situation, as this was the first frozen corpse they had ever found and delivered back to town.

When they pulled up to the Everet Hotel the gravel parking lot was filling up so they had to park the truck on an angle near the front door. The bar was on the right of the small lobby with a large picture window overlooking the vehicles parked outside. This was practical since everyone wanted to keep an eye on their vehicles to ensure that none had stalled. In these temperatures you could not turn off your engine unless you were going to plug in the block heater to ensure that the water in your radiator did not freeze, as well as the electric battery blanket, and with the cost of turbine-generated electricity the hotel was certainly not going to pay for thirty trucks to be plugged in and heated while the clientele drank themselves into oblivion.

So before Brian and Mary were even out of the cab, the locals were out on the hotel porch to greet them.

"What the hell is Johnny doing now?" came a voice from the group.

"Anything to attract an audience, eh?" Bob the owner of the inn was front and centre, standing with his hands on his hips and grinning.

"He's gonna freeze to death up there!" shouted Father O'Reilly.

"He already has!" Brian slammed the door of the truck.

Bob strode out to the pickup. "What the hell?"

"It's a long story and I need a beer!" Brian brushed past the innkeeper and headed into the bar.

"He's dead! He's frozen solid!"

"Yes he is Father," Mary put her arm around the priest's shoulders.

"I know he could be an asshole sometimes, but you didn't have to kill him!" piped in Eddie Harvey the owner of the only gas station in town.

"Very funny!" Brian glanced back over his shoulder, "Get me a beer!"

They left Johnny in the back of the truck and went into the bar to warm up and refresh their drinks. Everyone sat down at the window to look out again at the strange spectacle, and wait to hear the details of this Saturday night tale. This was going to be a good one, and they eagerly waited for Brian and Mary to join them.

Both Brian and Mary liked to tell a good story and sometimes they would frustrate each other trying to take centre stage, but Mary was too tired and cold to talk, so she sank into her chair to have one more look at Johnny and let Brian recount the day's events. Except for the odd exaggeration he did a pretty good job. She thought he could have toned down the parts where she was sitting on Johnny's chest with her ass in his face, but the audience certainly enjoyed it and she had to admit that if it had been someone else's rear end she would have found it outrageously funny.

It took Brian about an hour to recount every detail and the circle around them expanded steadily. By the time he had finished there were about twenty people shaking their heads and lamenting Johnny Michael's demise. After everyone had digested the news, a typical northern solution took shape and it was decided that a wake should be held with Johnny so all could say good-bye. Any excuse for a party was acceptable in this country. The trouble with the infamous northern perspective is that it is usually fuelled by alcohol, which results in decisions that are often deemed inappropriate by the more conservative outsider down south.

"We can't bring him inside, he'll thaw out and stink like hell," said Bob, "Have you ever smelled a rotting human body? That smell is a bitch to get rid of. Frank Smith had to finally burn his cabin down and rebuild after he found his wife dead when he came home from a week's fishing last summer."

"Okay then, we'll join him outside," came a suggestion from the gathering.

Without hesitation everyone rose, donned their parkas, grabbed a chair and a drink and went out on the hotel porch. They all sat down and stared at Johnny. After a few minutes Bob broke the silence, "This doesn't feel right. We can't leave him up there all alone."

With a few beers in him Brian agreed. "You're right. He needs to be down here with us in some sort of place of honour."

"He can't sit with us when his legs are stretched out like that. Are there any footstools around?" asked Father O'Reilly as he looked around the porch.

"The chairs have no arms, he'll just tip over all the time, believe me I know!" said Mary.

"You could sit on him," Brian smiled with a twinkle in his eye.

"Piss off!" retorted Mary.

"I know, I know, I know," stuttered Eddie, "we need the lounge chair my wife used last summer when she was trying to get a tan. She only used it once 'cause the damn mosquitoes drove her crazy!"

"Perfect! Go get it Eddie," yelled Bob as he went back into the hotel to get another beer.

With Eddie off to get the lounger, it was time for a watering and another drink. Everyone sauntered back into the hotel, happy for a little warmth while they waited for Eddie's return.

Bob was pleased. Saturday night was usually not so busy. His was a working man's bar and so it was later weekday evenings that were the busiest. Thursday night was best. After four days of work, and fighting either the cold or the mosquitoes, guys were ready for a drink and some relaxed conversation. With only a day or two left to work, Thursday night could see the place packed for hours. So this was a pleasant surprise.

Tonight was going to break some records for sure, both on the retail side and on the social side. He had not been expecting a wake!

People came in to the Everet Hotel for three reasons: to have a drink, to enjoy the company of others and to listen to Bob's story of the day. Bob was a natural tale-spinner and comedian and the hotel gave him a constant, attentive audience. Sometimes he reworked an old story and other times he embellished some insignificant current event, both required some thought and creativity to turn into the entertainment for which he was renowned. Rarely did a truly fantastic tale just drop in his lap. He was on sensory overload as he memorized every detail of the unfolding evening; Johnny's expression, the reactions of others and even the number of icicles on Johnny's chin.

"Here comes Eddie!" someone yelled and the whole crew moved out onto the porch once more.

Chapter Three

*T*he lounge chair was opened and Johnny Michael was placed on it. It was rather haunting to see him there, legs outstretched and crossed at the ankles, arms folded at the chest. Everyone grabbed a chair and settled down around the guest of honour.

"You'd swear to God he was just taking a nap!" observed Mary.

"Maybe that's all death is . . . just an extended nap," Brian closed his eyes and began to snore.

There was a long silence again as everyone had a drink and studied the guest of honour sitting with them. Someone commented on how peaceful he looked and another agreed that since we all have to die, this was a good way to go. Apparently freezing to death is ranked high as one of the more pleasant ways to die. Most people who die from temperature loss do not actually freeze because the outside temperatures are above zero.

People die of hypothermia when their body temperature falls somewhere below 80-70 degrees Fahrenheit. The normal body temperature of 98.5 only needs to drop one degree for shivers and discomfort to set in. Anywhere below that and the human brain starts producing all kinds of chemicals to fight off the cold and pain, amnesia at 93 degrees, apathy at 91 degrees and virtual stupor at 90 degrees. Ironically at about 85 degrees your body begins to feel uncomfortably hot and many hypothermia victims actually rip off their clothes in the final stages. This would not have been the case with Johnny. At sub-zero temperatures, the stages of hypothermia move quickly so he would have enjoyed simply falling into a stupor early on in the process. And that is certainly what it looked like now . . . Johnny was just relaxing on the lounger and catching a few winks while his friends enjoyed themselves.

"There's got to be more to it than that," muttered Eddie, "I mean nothing else in the universe just starts and then ends, why should we be any different?"

"Why do we even give a damn? Why can't people just enjoy life and take whatever comes, without so much worry about it?" Brian looked sardonically at the guest of honour.

"For the same reason that we're all up here in this godforsaken country, we're curious. Otherwise people would never accomplish anything. We'd all be napping constantly, like Johnny over there!" Bob raised his chin and thrust his nose in Johnny's direction.

"I don't know what happens when we kick the bucket, but I know what doesn't happen."

"And what's that Eddie?" asked Bob.

"We sure as hell don't end up in some green valley, sitting in white robes with angels playin' harps all around us. Sorry Father!"

"Doesn't bother me Eddie. I know where most of you are going to end up!" smiled Father O'Reilly.

"Now that's a fact!" laughed Bob. "Why do you think Father is always hangin' around with us? It can't be the stimulating conversation! He's trying to save a few souls!"

"Well he sure has his work cut out for him, eh?" Brian glanced fondly at the priest.

"Shouldn't we be worried about Johnny's soul at the moment? He's the one on the journey as we speak," philosophized Mary.

"Ahhhh, back to the 'journey' again," murmured Bob. "You know, most people are fools. I mean think about it . . . all this fascination with the afterlife. I think we look too hard. All the answers to any of the really big questions we've asked over the years were right here on earth. You know what I think happens when you die?" Everyone leaned forward and listened intently. "I think the first thing that you do is kick yourself in the ass and say . . . 'Why didn't I see it? It's so obvious! The answer was staring me in the face all along!"

"That's damn profound!" blasted Eddie.

"It's fuckin' brilliant that is!" added Brian.

A heavy silence fell over the group as each person stared out at the parking lot, each trying to see the 'obvious' that was supposedly staring them in the face. After a couple of minutes most had lost interest in the 'obvious' thought and were back to chatting about Johnny, only Father O'Reilly continued to stare off into the distance, but he was now asking himself a different question. What the hell was he doing, sitting here, on a sub-arctic hotel porch, drinking with a dead man? This had not been one of the duties that he had envisioned when coming out of the seminary. He came from a long Irish tradition of wakes, but there was something more than a little demented with this version. He knew that the powers to be in the bishop's office would not be impressed. Yet in another twist of nature, he knew that he understood these people and their take on life; furthermore he liked it!

The rawness was addictive. Yes, Johnny Michael was dead. Well . . . we die. That was the northern perspective. What was that old adage people always say with acceptance? Oh yes, 'there are three inevitable things in this world, life, death and taxes'. These days it seemed that many people in the south spent all their energy in an attempt to deny death. Last time he was south of sixty or 'out' as it was referred to in the Arctic, he had met two old parishioners in Vancouver and at one point in the conversation, one of them said, "Father, did you know that Colin Parker's grandmother died?"

"How old was she?" asked Father O'Reilly.

"Eighty-nine," was the answer.

The two friends continued with their own chat. "What did she die of?"

"Lung cancer!"

"Well she smoked all her life, foolish woman."

"We have to face the consequences of our own choices!"

"What can we expect, eh Father? We can't expect mercy, if we don't take care of our bodies."

Father O'Reilly always wanted to scream when he heard these kinds of conversations. What can we expect? She was eighty-nine years old for God's sake. At this point, what does it matter if she smoked, drank or ate a Mars Bar every hour? Eighty-nine years is a pretty good run!

The paradox of it all was that these guys on the porch lived life to the fullest. Not a day passed without friendship, laughter, good food and drink; all packaged in a very base acceptance of the fragility of life and an appreciation of each day that they survived. They enjoyed life and accepted death when it arrived. While 'outside' more and more people were jogging, eating bean sprouts, and following daily schedules of self-punishment to take as much joy out of living as possible, so they could live longer! What the hell was that all about?

He remembered Bob telling one of his stories a while back and had heard him saying, "Life, death and taxes, that sums it up. The difference with people up here is that we worry about what we can control. I haven't paid taxes for twenty years! Hopefully old man death will catch up with me before Revenue Canada does!"

The dilemma that Father O'Reilly always faced with these Everet parishioners was this: although they were all uniquely spiritual and believed in an afterlife, his ancient church description of eternal bliss did not entice them much. Eddie had once asked him to describe Hell, because he had been thinking that perhaps it might be a more enjoyable place to park his soul for eternity.

He felt accepted here. People did not just see him as the voice of baptisms and funerals or the purveyor of the sacraments. They expected him to be involved in all their special ceremonies and it seemed perfectly normal to everyone to be having a last drink with a dead man, in a tavern parking lot and chatting with Father O'Reilly about the situation.

·······················

Chapter Four

*T*he hotel parking lot was packed when Constable Jackson Pedley drove in and hopped out of his police pickup. The fog created by all the exhaust fumes was clouding his vision and he could see that there was some activity on the front porch, but he could not make out any details. It was too damn cold for so many people to be outside, something must be up. He made his way through the maze of trucks, trying to get a clearer image of the scene.

He was shaking his head and laughing to himself, "What the hell were those jerks doin' now? Look at Johnny Michael on that summer lounge chair. Too goddamn funny! It must be his birthday or somethin'".

He remembered his own birthday last winter, when everyone decided since he couldn't get off to Hawaii for a break that they would bring Hawaii to him. They had totally cleared out a friend's house and put in lounge chairs, a plastic kid's pool, paper palm trees and sunlamps. Everyone had dressed in bathing suits, tennis outfits and one guy even came in scuba diving gear. It had been great, except for the damn sunburn! He'd had red, pealing, itchy skin for weeks after that, but it had been worth the discomfort. What a blast!

Before he reached the group, he had been spotted by Brian who was hollering at him to come over and join them. "Jackson my man! Get on over here."

"Why wasn't I invited to this little get together?"

"Well it was kind of a spontaneous thing," said Bob, "We're calling it 'The Last Trupper'". He was already working on one-liners for tales to come.

"Johnny looks kind of bored with it all," observed Jackson.

"Well the company is a bit too full of life for his liking," continued Bob.

Everyone chuckled except Jackson who had now stepped up on the porch and was taking a good look at the guest of honour. Bob, with a twinkle in his eyes, was watching Jackson intently. This would surely be one of the funnier moments in the saga, the cop realizing that everyone was gathered around a corpse. Most of the others were too drunk and having too much fun to comprehend that this might be a problem for a law enforcement officer. Bob suspected that there were alternative ways to deal with a dead man, and this particular method would not be in Constable Pedley's official training manual from Ottawa. Yet Bob could not help thinking that this was probably the best damn way to deal with a death. Sit it right down in front of you, pay tribute and deal with it. No morbid hymns, no satin, no flowers, and most of all no undertaker arranging details, just honest lamenting done by sincere friends. Although Bob was not expecting Jackson to see it quite that way, he also was not expecting what was to follow.

Constable Jackson Pedley had walked over to the lounge chair. He had knelt down on one knee, had removed his right hand from his extremely warm and comfortable RCMP issue mitten and had placed it below Johnny's left jawbone to take his pulse. Now anyone who has grown up in a winter climate learns at a very early age not to place warm, moist flesh on anything that is frozen. Most kids find themselves at some point in their early years with a tongue or a hand stuck fast to a Popsicle, icicle or metal fence post. It is not a nice experience. Throughout any given winter, fire trucks can be seen pulling up to school yards in order to carefully and slowly remove extremities from frozen items. It has all got to do with the conduction of heat. Certain things conduct heat very well such as metal and water, so when a nice wet tongue, lip or hand touches an extremely cold piece of metal or ice, the cold item immediately takes the heat from the damp, warm body part and the moisture freezes in an instant, leaving the two bonded rock solid. It does not happen with rubber or wood, because they have a lower heat conduction level than people, who are more than seventy-five percent water. So after God knows how long, sitting frozen at that tree, Johnny was virtually a very cold icicle. Like any other well-rounded adult, Jackson knew this law of nature; the problem was he did not know that Johnny Michael was frozen solid. It was not until he began to rise from one knee that the harsh reality set in. His right hand was stuck like glue to Johnny's neck.

"Jesus Christ he's frozen solid! How long have you guys been sitting here?" screamed Jackson.

Brian leaned back on his chair and clasped his hands behind his head, "I know some of our parties can go on forever Pedley, but we've only been at this one for a couple of hours."

Everybody broke out in laughter and Eddie added, "He arrived that way."

"We're having a sort of farewell party for him," Brian said, "We're calling it 'The Last Trupper'."

Some one-liners have eternal life and this one got another round of hoots from the guests.

"No more details! Just get my hand off his goddamn neck!"

"Jesus, the last time my tongue was stuck to a metal post I was three years old. I don't remember what my mother did," Brian was leaning forward to study the situation.

"When it happened to me the fire department came and they had some special liquid, but I was four years old, I don't know what it was," shivers ran down Mary's spine as she recalled the pain.

"Maybe hot water would work," Father O'Reilly suggested.

Bob shook his head, "No good. It has to be boiling to work before it freezes and we'd scald Jackson's hand for sure."

While all the suggestions were being bandied about, Eddie had stood up and walked over the Johnny's neck. Just as Bob was pointing out the dangers of boiling water, Eddie unzipped his fly and urinated on Constable Jackson Pedley's hand. It worked like a charm and the hand was immediately freed of the corpse. Jackson was up in a flash, and jumping around holding his hand as far from his body as possible and screaming, "Jesus Christ, you just pissed on me! You pissed on my goddamn hand!" He was off the porch and into the hotel washroom before anybody else could say a word.

They could not have spoken anyway, shock and amusement held everyone in a form of suspended animation; no one could speak. Then one of those fantastic group laughs that bring tears to the eyes, redden ear lobes and cause some to double over trying to catch their breath took hold. Only Eddie was able to lean against the hotel wall and casually take a sip from his beer.

"It's obvious none of you work in a gas station! Sometimes when you're fixing an engine, you need bare hands. This happens all the time over there," Eddie told them.

"That's why you and your guys always stink!" stammered Brian, holding his nose and backing away from Eddie.

"Very funny!" Eddie feigned a few punches at his buddy.

"Well I guess we're in big shit now," Brian began to pace the porch. "We didn't call the police and when he did arrive someone pissed on him! Jesus Christ Eddie, I can't believe you did that!"

"Now we're not only sitting with a dead friend, but he has yellow icicles hanging from his hood!" Mary backed her chair away from the guest of honour.

Everyone was roaring again when Jackson came back on to the porch and said, "All right you idiots, the party's over!"

There were moans and groans from everyone, but most were actually ready to go to bed. Jackson made everyone leave in three-minute intervals. His logic being, that since the roads were empty, if they were far enough apart, there would be no accidents unless they simply drove into the snow bank. So it took about half an hour for the last of the guests to depart. Then he hopped in his truck and drove around town to ensure that everyone was home and safe inside their abodes. He had purposely kept Brian, Mary and Eddie back since he would need some help with the body. Of course Bob was also there to offer his services. When he returned to the hotel, Johnny was lounging on the porch alone, while the others had gone into the tavern to warm up and have a coffee.

It was about one in the morning and Jackson paused on the hotel porch to enjoy the view of the empty parking lot, with no exhaust fumes to cloud the scene. It was seriously cold tonight. After about forty below zero, it was hard to differentiate the temperatures, cold was cold, but a good measure was the smoke coming from each chimney. Until minus thirty-five degrees Fahrenheit it billows out in a cloudy pattern going in various directions, but below that temperature it streams straight up in a narrow line and no movement can be detected. That is what the constable could see on this chilly night; perhaps a hundred thin, still, perpendicular lines rising from every building. He stood gazing at the town for a few more minutes before he turned to the problem at hand, the frozen trapper.

I suppose it really didn't matter if these characters wasted a few hours without notifying him. Johnny Michael had obviously been dead for at least a week to be frozen that stiff, he thought to himself. He'd have to go out to the scene tomorrow with Brian and Mary to record details and write up a report, which would not include the wake on the hotel porch! Other than the spontaneous party, nothing else appeared out of the ordinary. This would be a standard report on a common form of death in these parts. At least one or two people froze to death every winter.

It used to be quite common to find a body frozen in the forest, but these days not too many people made a living off the land. It was more the norm to find someone in a vehicle on the highway, frozen at the wheel. If a car ran out of gas or broke down and it was early evening, chances were no other vehicle would pass for more than twelve hours. When someone had to travel at night it was accepted practice to tell the people at the destination the time of departure and the estimated time of arrival, so they could call the police if more than an hour passed and the expected guest had not arrived.

It was also common practice to carry at least twelve candles and a box of matches in the vehicle glove compartment. A candle will not keep a truck cab comfortable, but it will keep the temperature high enough to maintain life if someone is forced to wait for help to arrive.

Unfortunately, circumstances sometimes culminate with an unlucky traveller stopped on a lonely stretch of winter road without a friend awaiting the arrival or candles and matches in the glove box. It's a grim reminder of the fragility of life and the importance of minor preparations.

Mounties spent a good portion of their time on duty driving the Alaskan Highway and looking for stopped vehicles or worse, tire tracks going off the road and down embankments. Just last summer, Jackson had been out driving and had stopped to enjoy a particularly impressive view on one of the thousands of sharp curves the highway offered. He had his binoculars out and was scanning the mountainside for wild mountain goats when he happened to look down below him and spotted what looked like a car fender. Two days later, they finally were able to hoist the car up and onto the road. It was an old Buick with Illinois licence plates from 1956. The vehicle held the skeletal remains of a man, a woman and a child. The details of the incident were recorded with photos and endless reports, and then the human remains and paperwork was sent off to FBI headquarters in Chicago. It would probably be an open file forever. In 1956 people did not use credit cards, so it was hard to trace movement. Middle class people were not accustomed to telephoning long distance and often people going north in those days did not even tell others where they were heading. Usually it was to begin a new life or run away from some difficult situation.

Eighteen years later in the summer of 1974, when Jackson Pedley found the old Buick, forensic science did not include DNA testing or any of the other advanced techniques that were to aid investigations by the turn of the century. He had tried to lift a few fingerprints off the interior of the car. It was obvious that they had not all died on impact, because the moisture created by at least one of the passengers breathing inside the closed chamber had created dampness and everything had been washed clean in the last few hours after the tragic accident so many years earlier.

This particular incident had haunted Jackson for the rest of the summer and into the autumn. Usually skeletal remains were easier to deal with than flesh and blood, but in this case, the child's remains were found huddled on the woman's lap. That in itself was not upsetting, but being an investigator, Jackson had also noticed that the woman's arms were not around the child. So he had determined that the mother had probably died first, and the poor child had crawled onto his dead mother's lap before dying. The scene of a small child sobbing on his dead mother's knee and slowly dying would wake Jackson from a sound sleep for years. It is odd the memories that eat at the brain and the ones that are easily forgotten. Jackson would have been about the same age as this unknown child in 1956, so while he was playing with his brothers in Winnipeg, this poor kid was sobbing on his Mommy's knee and begging her to wake up. Pedley had seen far more gruesome and severe accidents, yet this one had stuck and would not be released until the unconscious side of his mind made the decision. Jackson would have to deal with the memory of this child until his brain had processed it and come to terms with its meaning and worth to him.

A tap on the tavern window broke the silence, and his thoughts. He turned to see Brian waving at him to come inside. He took another quick glance at Johnny then went into the bar to sit with the others.

"What were you doing out there for so long?" inquired Brian. "It's too damn cold to be loitering around."

"Just thinking about Johnny and whether he has a mother."

"I think that I can say unequivocally that he definitely has a mother!" Brian smiled.

"You know what I mean. He wasn't that old, what . . . maybe forty. There's a good chance she's still alive. Must be awful to lose a child," Jackson sat down with a coffee.

Bob was topping up everyone's brew. "It's not nice when life doesn't play by the rules is it? Parents are supposed to be the first to go otherwise it must be gut-wrenching. We never love our parents the way we love our children. It's a cruel world that takes a child first."

"Well we'll know soon enough won't we? I'll need to write up everything tomorrow and I also need to take you two back to the scene so I can complete all the forms. I swear this job is ninety percent paperwork!" groaned Jackson.

Mary and Brian looked at each other, both dreading the trek back in to the scene.

"That's all fine and dandy," added Bob as he set the coffee pot back on the hot plate, "but what about right now? What do you want to do with the body? I don't need him greeting customers for breakfast in five hours!"

Mary turned to Bob, "That would make for a few more stories,"

"Now Mary, don't go and take things too far and ruin it for everybody!" This was one of Brian's favourite lines when he was joking around with friends.

"I know, I know. I have a tendency to go to the extreme. Thank God you're always around to hold me back," Mary often used sarcasm when dealing with her partner.

"That's what keeps us together Babe. You're so unstable and I'm so sane."

Jackson ignored the sparring of his two friends, "I've got to get him into a body bag, and then into the freezer at the station."

As he spoke he suddenly realized that he had a serious problem. The RCMP freezer served as the local morgue. Bodies needed to be held somewhere official and besides that, no one could be buried in the winter months because the ground was rock hard. Even a small, coffin sized hole could not be dug until mid-spring, so bodies were kept in the makeshift morgue until then. Pedley's office had only one freezer, as he never accumulated more than three bodies in any given winter, and his freezer held three corpses quite nicely, one stacked upon the other. He already had one individual in the freezer and that was now creating a problem. If the freezer had been empty, then Johnny could have been placed inside sitting up, but with one body already inside, the freezer would not close unless Johnny was lying down, as a normal corpse should.

He explained this to everyone and Eddie offered a suggestion. "Something like this happened a few years back," he said, "Sheila Capp froze to death in her truck just north of the junction. The Mounties couldn't fit her in the freezer. Besides that, we all decided that it just didn't seem right to have a corpse in any position other than lying flat, just seemed more dignified to be lying down. A body bag looks pretty weird all bent up in a sitting position! Sooner or later the corpse has to go into a coffin and into the ground."

"So what did they do?" Jackson was hoping to find a viable solution.

"You've been through quite a lot tonight Jackson. Are you sure you want to know?" Bob grimaced over his coffee cup.

"No I'm not sure! But I've got a corpse sitting out on the porch of this hotel on a lounge chair and I've got to do something in the next four hours before this turns into a Martin and Lewis movie! What did you do with Sheila Capp's body to flatten her out?"

"It only took about thirty minutes, start to finish. Wouldn't you say Bob?"

"And it really wasn't as bad as it sounded later," the two men nodded in agreement.

"It was the best decision under the circumstances," continued Eddie.

"Good Lord, if you two can't even spit it out, it must be up there in your top ten repertoires of

Everet outrageous events," Mary walked over to
the window to check on Johnny.

Bob thought for a moment and then bellowed,
"By God I think it might top the list!"

"Weirdest thing I ever did!" Eddie
murmured.

"The clock is tickin' guys. Spit it out,"
demanded Jackson.

"I think it's best if we just do it. If we talk
about it first you young guys will wimp out," Bob
stood up and put on his parka.

"He's right. Let's go. When the going gets
tough, the tough get going! Come on outside.
Let's give these young punks a little life experience, eh Bob?" Eddie was a little more emphatic
than his usual self. He was obviously trying to
prime himself up for a challenging deed.

"Jackson, you and Brian each grab a couple
of cement blocks from the side of the hotel. Four
blocks should be all we need," instructed Bob.

Eddie and Bob were out on the porch and
picking Johnny's body up before the others could
zip up their parkas and go for the cement blocks.
By the time Jackson, Brian and Mary were out
of the hotel, Bob and Eddie were halfway across
the parking lot and placing Johnny on the ground
with his feet up against the only lamp post in the
area. Brian and Pedley grabbed the blocks and
ran to catch up with them.

The two older men were walking toward
Eddie's gas station when the other three arrived
at the spot. They were standing there, silently

studying the corpse which was lying on its side, when Bob returned with a heavy rope. He took the cement blocks and placed two on each side of Johnny, so he was sitting up again and facing the post. Then he knelt down and began to tie Johnny's ankles securely to the base of the lamp post. "There! That should do it." said Bob, standing up again. "Ready Eddie!" He hollered.

Jackson was about to ask just what they were ready for, when a loud roar broke the silence. At three in the morning without a vehicle on the road or a person on the street, Eddie's backhoe made a horrendous racket. It came out of the station's garage slowly, but then turned and came towards the group amazingly quickly. It was not until the old, yellow machine was bouncing along over the parking lot that Brian and Mary realized that Eddie was going to use this monster to flatten Johnny. They looked to Jackson for a reaction, but the officer had already turned his back and was walking towards his police truck. Brian ran to catch up with him, while Mary stayed with Johnny.

"Where are you going Jackson? You can't just leave!"

"Of course not! I'm getting the body bag out of my supply box." Jackson was already up on the box of his truck, and opening the large container that ran along the back of his cab wall. He tossed the folded black bag at Brian and then locked up his supply case again.

As he jumped off the truck, he took the bag from Brian and walked back toward the others.

When they were back at the site, the backhoe was slowly positioning itself behind Johnny's back.

Although Mary and Brian were to be witnesses to this bizarre scene, they never could get a clear view of the actual 'flattening' when they tried to recollect the scene. They were cold and tired. They had been up for almost twenty-four hours and they had been drinking heavily at the wake. They were both physically and mentally numb.

"Ready?" Bob looked at Jackson.

Jackson nodded at Bob. Bob nodded at Eddie. Eddie nodded back to Bob. He gently lifted the arm of the backhoe, folded the shovel of the hoe up so he could use the back of the scoop and raised the arm, moving the scoop over Johnny's head and resting the back of the scoop on Johnny's lap. Then he slowly and gently manoeuvred the scoop towards the backhoe pushing the corpse into a lying position. One final little tap on Johnny's chest and it was over.

As the backhoe trotted off back to the gas station, Jackson and Bob quickly placed Johnny in the black body bag and zipped it up. Jackson shouted at Brian to help him carry the body to his truck and Bob untied the rope and walked over to the station. The roar of the backhoe still filled the night air, as Brian and Jackson left in the police truck to deliver the body to the police freezer, and Bob entered the gas station.

When Eddie turned off the machine, the silence was almost deafening. Mary stood alone at the lamp post digesting what she had just witnessed. She was gazing silently across the parking lot when she tilted her head to look at the night sky. That's when she saw it. There on top of the lamp post was the largest, most majestic snow owl she had ever seen. He was a metre high and sat silently looking down on her.

Snow owls are magnificent creatures and few people are ever privileged enough to see one. Mary had heard the odd story of a trapper or prospector seeing one, and sometimes even a parliament of them, always on a very cold winter's night and always in an isolated location. She had never heard of a sighting in town. This silent, almost fluorescent white bird sat motionless on its perch. Its enormous round eyes were penetrating Mary, but it was not disconcerting, it was soothing. Mary suddenly realized that she was crying. She stared at the owl as it silently spread its wings and glided away. She smiled and wiped her tears with the arm of her parka. Ecstasy, joy, pain, agony, there was nothing placid about this place she called home.

II

The International
Curling Stone Incident

Chapter Five

$\mathcal{I}$t was pitch black outside when Mary turned off
her alarm and rolled out of bed. It was always
night when you woke during an Arctic winter. The
sun would eventually rise and move in a small
circle on the horizon for a few brief hours at mid-
day, but basically December and January days ran
together into one very long evening. People kept
busy with a variety of indoor projects, and limited their excursions to the drive back and forth
to work. The drive to work at minus forty degrees
Fahrenheit required enough planning and energy
to fill the first few hours of each day.

Mary turned on the kettle and then slipped
into her boots, zipped up her parka and ran outside
to start up her small Datsun truck. She was the
first in town to own one of the new little foreign
vehicles. It was actually made by Nissan, but in
those days Japanese automobile companies were
not household names, and no one would have

been very interested in the manufacturer. Initially everyone had had a good laugh when she drove it up from Edmonton, but they had all become more interested in the vehicle as she tallied her gasoline bills over the winter. The first few Japanese cars looked out of place sitting beside the huge American counterparts, but it did not take long for paradigms to shift as owners reported the huge savings. The additional advantage was the smaller cab which heated up in half the time compared to the huge interiors of the Ford and GM vehicles.

Mary turned the key and the truck started on the first try. She left the three electrical cords hanging out of her front grill plugged into the house. Even after the truck started, it was important to leave it running for at least half an hour until it was completely warmed up before unplugging any electrical lifelines. She ran back into the warmth of the house to have her first cup of tea and wake up.

Brian was up a few minutes later and donning his boots and jacket to greet his truck. His day did not begin as well as Mary's did and she could hear him cursing outside. When she looked out the window she saw that his truck had started, but Brian was still sitting in the freezing cab. She realized what had happened and shook her head in sympathy.

Virtually all vehicles in Everet were standard transmission. If the battery died, the truck could be pushed downhill and started again; if it got stuck in the snow or spring mud it was easier to rock back and forth or shift into lower gears to bulldoze out, and Eddie could repair a standard faster and cheaper. The only downside of a standard truck was demonstrated on very cold winter mornings if the driver had forgotten to put the truck in neutral before shutting down the night before. At extremely cold temperatures the gears could not be shifted until the engine had warmed up significantly which usually took twenty to thirty minutes. If the truck had been left in gear, this meant that the driver had to sit in the cab, in freezing temperatures, with his foot on the clutch, until things had warmed up enough to shift into neutral and leave it idling. It was not a pleasant way to begin the day.

Mary poured Brian a hot cup of coffee and brought it, along with a blanket, out to him.

"Thanks Babe," he muttered, "how could I be so stupid? We need to put a big sign on the wall of the house that says 'Put truck in neutral!'"

"That's not a bad idea," she replied. "Sorry hon, I'd love to chat, but I'm going back inside."

By the time Brian was able to leave his truck idling in neutral and come back in the house, Mary was already dressed for work and on her second cup of tea. He poured a fresh cup of coffee and joined her at the kitchen table.

"Well that was a great way to wake up! Hope the rest of my day goes better," he stared at his swirling coffee and warmed his hands on the steaming cup.

"At least it's Friday. It's easier to handle something like this at the end of the week. Imagine if you'd been sitting out there on a Monday morning," comforted Mary.

"No kidding. I'd have to kill you," said Brian.

"That's nice. You forget to put your truck in neutral, so you decide to kill me!" Mary flicked his arm with her finger.

"When you're outside, half asleep, sitting in a freezing cab all sanity is lost. Looking at your truck warming up on its own and thinking of you inside the nice warm house waking up slowly, is enough to drive anyone right over the edge. There's only one thing that saved you from certain death," he murmured slyly.

"And what may I ask was that?" Mary looked up in mock horror.

"I couldn't take my foot off the goddamn clutch and come in to get you!" he leaned over and gave her a peck on the cheek.

"Thank God for small mercies!" she raised her eyes to the ceiling, as she rose to go and put on her makeup in the bathroom.

"What are we doing tonight?" he called from the kitchen.

"I don't know. I'm still digesting everything from last weekend. I can't say that Johnny Michael was a close friend, but between the hiking, the wake and the backhoe, I'm still a little shook up. Do you mind if I just come home and curl up with a book?"

"Of course not. Jackson asked if we wanted to meet him at the hotel for supper, so I'll give him a call and tell him he'll be stuck with me tonight. And sometime after that I have to load up the truck with the beer cases, so I won't be home till later."

As Mary came out of the bathroom, she added, "Don't forget to leave your truck in neutral tonight when you get home!"

"Cute . . . very cute!"

Just as Mary was getting ready to face the great outdoors, the telephone rang. Brian was still enjoying his coffee as he reached across the table to answer it.

Picking up the receiver he greeted the caller with "Hell's kitchen!"

Mary silently threw him a kiss and went out to her truck. After she unplugged all three extension cords from the vehicle and wrapped them neatly around the plug-in post so she would be able to find them easily if it snowed during the day, she hopped into the cab. She was busy thinking of her classes and what she was going to do with her students to help them finish their poetry projects as she backed out of the driveway.

Brian was busy thinking also, but his thoughts were a little less mundane. The phone call had been rather extraordinary. Jackson had called in a panic and asked Brian to get over to the station pronto. He had not offered any details on the phone, just told Brian that he needed his help right away. So Brian threw on his clothes and rushed out the door. It would only take him a few minutes to reach the RCMP station. He was glad that he had started his truck up early and was able to respond to Jackson's call quickly. In this hostile land it was not good to leave a friend in distress for very long.

•◦•◦•◦•◦•◦•◦•◦•◦•◦•◦•◦•◦•

Chapter Six

*T*he nice thing about a small northern town is that everyone is involved in the daily running of the community. People do not have to listen to police bands, or wonder where the fire truck is off to, or peek out their living room windows to spy on neighbours. Everybody knows everything. Most of the adults in town operate all the necessary businesses for daily existence, as well as serving on the municipal council, the volunteer fire department, the school board, the recreation board and all the other various and sundry committees that enable people to function as a social group.

Brian was part of this community process. He was a volunteer fire fighter and president of the curling club. The Everet Curling Club was one of the larger organisations in town. The club owned its own building which held six sheets of ice and an observation room at one end, where spectators could have a drink and enjoy the games. A standard sheet of ice is 140 feet by 15 feet, with a target painted at each end of the curling lane. The target is 12 feet in diameter and is painted red and blue. The sheets run parallel to each other, with only a narrow piece of wood dividing the lanes. At one end, the wall behind the targets is usually glassed, so people can sit and watch all the games being played simultaneously. It is also a place to warm up, as the ice area is not heated. Forty pound, granite stones are released and slid from one end of the ice to the other end by teams of four, with the winning team having the most stones closest to the centre of the target. The game originated in Scotland and was introduced to Canada by early settlers. In the early 1970s, it was still only enjoyed and understood by the Scots and Canadians who spent endless winter hours at local clubs, curling and/or drinking; the other national pastime of both nations.

The club was most proud of its ninety-six beautiful stones made of Ailsa Craig Common Green granite which had come straight from Kays of Scotland. Although most club members were hardy drinkers, it had taken the club five years to raise the twenty thousand dollars, and another year waiting for the stones to arrive. In true Scot tradition, each member had ordered that extra drink for the road after each game, in order to aid the 'stone' fund. Not many clubs north of sixty could boast of such fine stones. The annual bonspiel brought teams from all over the north, many of them anxious to play a game with proper stones, rather than large cans, filled with water and frozen solid.

Mary came from a long line of avid Northern Ontario curlers and had been introduced to the game almost from birth, when she would sit on a family member's knee and watch her parents, grandparents, or other extended family curling. She started curling herself at thirteen and so by the time she and Brian had met, she was an expert team leader and strategist, taking the role of team 'skip'. Brian had not started curling until after high school and was bottom man on the team as the 'lead'. In true Scottish tradition the team members are all equally as valuable, but much of the strategy is left to the two senior team members, the skip and vice-skip. Brian appreciated this aspect, as he could enjoy the game and socialise, leaving Mary and Father O'Reilly to discuss the more serious aspects of any particular game.

An average game lasts about two hours, so Brian and Mary could play a game, enjoy the mandatory after game drink with the team they had played against, and still be home by 9:30 or 10:00 on a weeknight. It was their winter obsession and gave the couple a common denominator for conversation and friendship, which strengthened their relationship.

Brian was busy analysing his game from the previous night. His shots had been too light and half of his stones had not reached the mandatory 'hog line' which meant they were removed from play. In typical curling fashion, no one had dwelled on his missed shots, but it still bothered him and he decided that he would stop by the club later in the day and throw a few practice rounds so he could read the ice better for the next game. He was still replaying the game in his mind when he pulled up to the police station.

Jackson was at his desk when Brian entered the small office. "Thank God you're here. I need your help. Early this morning someone broke into the curling club and stole twenty stones."

"What!" Brian moaned as he sat down opposite Pedley. "Why? Even though they cost a fortune, they're of no value to anyone else. It's not like there's a black market for granite curling stones."

"Well you're the president. Did you make arrangements for some stones to be polished or somethin'?"

"No. We do all the maintenance at the club during the summer months, when it's not in use. Who found the stones missing?"

"Bob did. He was on his way down to the hotel early this morning and remembered that he had forgotten his hat at the club last night and stopped by at 5:30 to pick it up. He glanced at the ice and noticed that one of the sheets had no stones. Then he noticed that the back door at the far end of the ice was open. He took a count and found twenty stones had disappeared. He didn't want to wake you unnecessarily, so he left the message with me. I thought I'd let you sleep another hour before calling."

"Let's get over there and take a look," Brian jumped up and was out the door in a flash.

"We'll need to take both trucks. I've got to run out to the airport after we look around the club," Jackson yelled as he grabbed his keys off the nail at the front door.

Brian was studying the back door to the club when Jackson pulled up. "Strange," he called to the Mountie, "No damage to the door at all. Either they had a key or the door wasn't locked up last night."

"Who has a key?" asked Jackson.

"Just about everybody! There's never been any reason for much security. We lock up the booze in the storage room, but other than that a lot of people come and go from here. It's nice to drop in and practice a few shots when you have some free time. Although you obviously don't know that Jackson, judging by the rocks you throw. There's nothing of much value except the liquor."

"And the curling stones!" Jackson was crouched down and studying the snow for evidence.

"Yeah, but they aren't of any value if they're not on the ice. It's not like you can use them at home or pawn them at the hotel for a drink. And they weigh about forty pounds each! Whoever took them has half a ton of granite in their truck!" Brian said.

"So we can assume that the thieves were in a pickup truck," calculated Jackson.

"How so?" asked Brian.

"Think about it, bud. Half a ton of stones… half ton pickup. They took what their truck would carry," Jackson was crouched and brushing the snow with his finger.

"Well that narrows it down to just about everybody in the country!" Brian kicked at the side of the building.

"At least we can eliminate the three car owners in town. Listen I'm gonna stick around here for awhile and check for tread marks, but with no damage to the door, there won't be much evidence. Then I'll ask the early birds in town if they saw anything unusual this morning."

"I've gotta get to work before Jim wonders what's up," Brian opened the door of his truck. "Give me a call if you find out anything that might give us a lead."

Brian veered his truck in a full circle and drove off to the propane company to start his day. Like almost every business in town, TranGas Propane was located on the Alaskan Highway. The highway was the main street in Everet and the town basically ran along each side of the road for about a kilometre. The grocery store, the hotel, the church, the gas station, the propane company, the hardware store, the little Chinese restaurant and a few summer souvenir shops all sat side by side along its borders.

Brian worked with three other men at Tran-Gas. It was an important business in Everet. A lot of vehicles ran on propane. It was cheaper than gas and a truck could carry quite a large tank up in the back of its box, so it was not necessary to fill up very often. There was a pump outside the front office where trucks pulled in to fill up. They also had two big tank trucks for deliveries. Many homes and buildings used propane for heat or for their appliances and hot water tanks. It was more reliable, and cheaper than electricity. In the summer they usually hired a couple of teenagers to work the pumps. Every tourist who pulled into town needed to fill all the tanks on their motor homes and they usually wanted a safety check or needed some sort of repair to equipment before heading back up the highway.

The TranGas facilities were the most modern in town; two big brick buildings and a massive storage tank to one side. It was a company based in Edmonton and they had built one of their standard, easily recognizable shops. Product branding was important, even on a frontier. Brian had worked there since he arrived in Everet. He had just written his gas exams last summer and received his official ticket, so he worked alongside the manager, Jim Donnelly. It was a good job. Some days could be slack, but then you made up for it with hours of overtime when something went wrong. Propane is serious business when problems arise, and the staff needed to know exactly what they were doing if a home had a problem. As Jim often said, "Propane is very safe . . . until it isn't!"

"Sorry I'm late Jim. Had a problem at the curling club this morning," Brian stamped his feet to dislodge the snow from his boots, as he grabbed a cup of coffee.

"What happen, the ice melt?"

"I wish!" Someone has taken off with twenty of our stones."

"That's more than a little strange! So is Jackson hot on the trail of the granite grabbers?"

"He would be, if there was a trail. I can't for the life of me figure out why someone would steal our curling stones."

"Me neither," an odd look began to transform Jim's face, "unless it's a vendetta my friend."

"Who would have a vendetta against . . . oh shit!" Brian suddenly realized what had happened, as he looked at Jim, who was nodding his head and trying to control a massive grin from forming on his face. "You think the guys in Boulder are still pissed off about last winter's bonspiel?"

"Oh I don't know . . . they go out to play their final games and every one of their brooms has only two or three strands of straw on them. Plucked bare . . . what a shame! Some kind of Dutch straw disease I guess," reminisced Jim as he put his feet on his desk and crossed his legs.

"You think they know it was us?"

"Well, ten Everet guys laughing so hard that they were pissing their pants would be a clue! They took it in their stride, but I'm sure they haven't forgotten. It's a long, dark winter with plenty of time to plan for revenge."

"Those sons of bitches! Okay, we need to call a meeting, 5 o'clock, hotel, be there!" commanded the club president as he went out to his truck to make his morning deliveries.

Chapter Seven

The sun had already set, as Brian pulled up to the hotel and got out of his truck. He met Father O'Reilly walking over from the parish.

"So, Brian, the Boulder boys have pulled a fast one on us."

"Yes they have Father. Yes they have!"

Bob, Eddie and Jim were already enjoying a drink when Brian and the priest entered the lounge. They joined them at the corner table and called for a round to Bob's wife Sandra, who was working the bar. Once everyone was settled and watered, Brian looked around the table. "It didn't take Jim long to figure out who took the stones last night. It had to be the Boulder crew."

"Well it's not like they didn't owe us one after the broom incident."

"I know, I know," Brian took a swig of his beer and leaned forward.

"We did buy everyone new brooms after the bonspiel," Eddie's sincerity was almost childlike.

"Yea, but that was after we won the A and B events. Damn, I can still see that short, funny guy dusting the ice with his handkerchief trying to bring the last stone in a few more inches!" Father O'Reilly wiped the froth from his mouth, "He fought the good fight, that's for sure."

"I thought they took it pretty well, but obviously the bastards have been plotting for months," Bob closed his eyes slightly and nodded his head with evil fervour. "Now we have to plan our retribution . . . AND get our stones back!"

"Should I give Jackson a call?" the priest rose to go to a telephone. "He may enjoy this."

"I don't think so Father," Brian cautioned, "This calls for devious and drastic measures. We don't want to compromise our only cop. Better if he finds out after the fact."

They ordered another round and began the brainstorming session. They all agreed that every member of the club had to be told to keep quiet and not talk about the missing stones. Offering no public acknowledgement of the theft would throw off the Boulder contingency and keep them on edge. They would know for sure that revenge was being planned if there was silence from Everet, and that in itself was half the fun. Bob was in seventh heaven. He was still getting mileage out of the Johnny Michael story and already another tale was developing. Frozen friends, stolen curling stones, revenge . . . he couldn't wait for the plans to take shape!

His friends did not let him down and by midnight they had an idea worked out. Brian went to load up his truck with beer cases and everyone else went home to sleep and to enjoy the dreams of Boulder and curling stones and the following night's events. It was going to be great. Another memorable and historic moment in Everet history!

Boulder was about two hundred kilometres, or one hundred and twenty miles from Everet. In winter that meant a four hour drive if the weather was good. So the Everet Curling Club Boulder Retribution Crew would have to plan for eight hours of driving time, there and back, as well as the time they would require in Boulder to complete the deed. They had decided that four pickups were needed, with four men in each truck.

They gathered the team at the TranGas office on Saturday and swore the entire group to secrecy. This was important business, so everyone agreed that not even wives or girlfriends would be told about the plan. A sixteen member team was already large, if they told others it could quickly turn into a hundred people with knowledge of the plan and then security would be seriously compromised.

It was decided that two trucks would drive through Boulder and a further forty kilometres up the highway then work from the far end back to town. The other two trucks would begin their work about forty kilometres before Boulder. Each group of two trucks had the same tasks and estimated that they could complete the mandate in about four hours. Maps and grids were drawn, numbers crunched, and lists made of equipment that would be needed.

They decided to call each other about three o'clock in the afternoon and each would pretend that he had a small emergency at work. This would enable them to rush out of their houses without any questions being asked by families. They would be on the road by three thirty and at their destinations by seven thirty on the first side and eight thirty on the far side.

The weather was cooperating. It was another sub-zero afternoon and that fitted well into the plan. In the middle of winter, on cold evenings, people do not venture far from town, so the roads leading to Boulder would be empty by six o'clock.

The first two trucks pulled off to the side of the road on the Everet side of Boulder, at the first Ministry of Transport (MOT) sign, reading *Boulder 30 miles.* They waved the other two trucks on and hopped out of their cabs to begin work. Out came the four ladders and the small generator and power tools. Four men were up on the ladders, at each post of the road sign, front and back. Two men positioned themselves between both posts to help grab the sign. Another team member stood waiting to hold on to the large nuts and bolts that would be passed to him. The last man stood on the road to act as a look out and warn of any vehicles approaching.

The operation went very smoothly, and they had the sign off, turned upside down and securely back up on the posts within twenty minutes. All the equipment was put back in the trucks; the ground was shovelled and then swept to cover all tracks. They took a moment to enjoy their work and have a laugh, before moving on to the next sign. By eleven o'clock every sign leading up to Boulder from Everet was upside down. They drove quietly through Boulder to meet up with the two trucks working the other side of town. They had made good time also and it took the four trucks no time at all to finish up the task. Then they drove back through Boulder, leaving about five hundred metres between each truck so as not to draw attention and began the four hour journey back to Everet.

As they were driving back the weather warmed up and it began to snow. That luscious light snow made up of huge floating snowflakes. They were only about half an hour out of Everet, so although it slowed the driving the men were thrilled.

"There is a God!" Father O'Reilly made the sign of the cross.

"Father's had an epiphany!" Bob turned on the windshield wipers and leaned forward to see the road more clearly.

But they all knew what the priest had really meant. By morning the signs would be covered with beautiful fresh snow, and better than that, any trace of their tampering would be erased permanently. All that would be left were about twenty-five signs, all upside down, leading into Boulder from either direction. It was perfect!

"I don't want to put a damper on this fine evening and our fantastic work guys, but enjoy your sleep tonight, because when the town of Boulder wakes up tomorrow morning and they realize what we've done, I suspect there'll be something in the works," Brian was loving the entire experience.

"No rest for the wicked!" Eddie smiled smugly as they pulled into town.

Chapter Eight

It was Sunday morning around eleven when everyone finally gathered at the Everet Inn, some for brunch in the small restaurant, but most for drinks in the much larger bar. It was a beautiful sunny day, like the days of late March and April, unusual for December. Almost everyone had been out during the morning hours either cross-country skiing or just walking and perhaps taking a few photos. On such days, there's a glistening spectacle called hoarfrost which makes for fantastic photographs. It occurs when the ground is very cold, but the air has warmed up significantly. Anywhere the warm air has created some moisture is a good breeding ground for this marvellous miracle of nature. The moisture forms into millions of delicate miniature spikes on items containing any small hint of dampness. Mary had taken hundreds of photos of this hoarfrost, planted on door knobs, growing on boots left outside and once, even placed artistically on a pile of fresh moose droppings. She had taken a unique shot that afternoon of a pair of jeans hanging on a clothesline. The jeans were frozen solid and covered in millions of sparkling spiky ice thorns. She was sitting with Bob and Sandra trying to describe the moment that she hoped she had captured with her 35mm Pentax, when Brian and Jim came over to join their table.

"Sleeping Beauty has arisen," murmured Mary while she twisted and played with the curls that framed her face.

"He's not the only one! Bob is usually up at the crack of dawn, and he didn't budge until nine this morning, which is like noon for normal people," Sandra winked at her man.

"What were you guys up to last night, poker?" asked Mary.

"No way," said Brian.

"I don't believe you!" retorted Mary.

"God I wish we had television up here!" Sandra commented, "At least if they were stuck to a TV we'd know what they were up to!"

"You're right Sandra. This country gives them way too much free time and that usually means some sort of mischief. Their brains, regardless of the size, have nothing to dull them. It'd be much better if they were glued to a screen and we knew where they were, and then we could relax and enjoy ourselves."

"Hardy, har, har!" said Brian. My brain is no smaller than yours! It's just that I have more important things weighing on my grey matter than hoarfrost forming on a pair of frozen blue jeans!"

"Touché," nodded Jim, "You ladies have absolutely no idea the stress we are under at the moment!"

"And what might that be?" asked Sandra.

"Never you mind. You'll find out soon enough when the shit hits the fan!" whispered Brian.

"What have you done now?" Mary began rubbing her forehead and looking down at the table.

"Nothing that wasn't absolutely necessary to uphold our honour and our pride," Brian straightened his back and puffed out his chest.

As the women began interrogating Brian, Bob and Jim, Jackson Pedley was in his office completing his weekly paperwork and reports that needed to be sent out to Whitehorse. Nothing much had happened in the past week except for the curling stone incident, and the club had not filed any official complaint since they felt at this point that it was part of an elaborate practical joke initiated by the Boulder Curling Club.

He had left his typewriter and was pouring his last cup of coffee for the day, when the phone rang. It was a Staff Sergeant Wilson calling from Ottawa. Constable Pedley did not receive many calls, if any, directly from the heart of the nation, so the call certainly peaked the officer's interest. The curiosity did not last long, and in a few moments Jackson was sitting at his desk, head lowered and resting on his free hand, while he shook his head slowly.

"The visit will only last a few hours," the staff sergeant was explaining, "They don't want anyone to know they are coming in. Keep it low profile. They'll be dressed casually. You just need to give them a quick tour of town, show them the sights and you know . . . give them a feel for the country. Don't worry about meals, they'll eat in Whitehorse. I know it's a bother constable, but it is part of the job. Public relations are a big part of our role. I'll send you a fax now with all the details. Oh and Constable, you understand of course, that you'll have to don the 'Serge'. I assume you have it pressed and your High-Browns polished at all times."

"Of course, sir," answered Jackson as he thought about his Red Serge uniform pushed back in the corner of his small closet, behind his fishing gear and the leather riding boots in a box somewhere in his bedroom.

The staff sergeant hung up and Jackson leaned back in his office chair and looked up at the ceiling. Five important Japanese government officials dropping in to tour Everet and get a 'feel' for the north! How was he supposed to guide a group of Asian politicians around town, while he was dressed in his Red Serge and keep it low profile? Headquarters doesn't have a clue what happens up here, Jackson shook his head as he glanced at his bedroom door and imagined the state of his dress uniform.

The RCMP or Royal Canadian Mounted Police have been a part of Canadian history since the inception of the country. Their predecessor was the North-West Mounted Police (NWMP) which was formed in 1873 when Canada's first Prime Minister, Sir John A. Macdonald decided that a special force was needed to ensure law and order prevailed in the expanding western territories (modern day Alberta and Saskatchewan) and to keep the Yankees at bay. In 1904, King Edward VII, in appreciation of the fine service of this para-military organization conferred the 'royal' prefix to the name and they became the Royal Northwest Mounted Police (RNWMP).

It was not until 1920 that the modern force of today began to evolve. The name was changed to Royal Canadian Mounted Police and their mandate became the federal policing of the entire nation.

The scarlet Red Serge riding uniform has been a symbol of the force since its inception. Mounties do not wear this uniform for regular duty. It is saved for formal functions such as an officer's wedding, RCMP Regimental banquets or as a display for dignitaries to symbolize the defence of the nation and national boundaries. Only a handful of officers wear this beautiful but uncomfortable uniform every day, and they are the young men stationed in Ottawa, on Parliament Hill. They patrol the house of government and stand for endless photos with tourists during each shift. Even the fellows on the famous

RCMP Musical Ride or in the RCMP Orchestra only wear the Serge during performances. Constable Pedley had not worn his Red Serge since his graduation ceremony in Regina five years earlier.

The irony of the Red Serge is that it is issued upon graduation. After the intensive training that a young man received in those days, he graduated in the best physical shape of his life. The buff, healthy, strong young men on parade at the graduation ceremony look magnificent in the newly issued Red Serge. They say their sad farewells to members of their training groups and then disperse throughout the nation with postings from Vancouver to Halifax to Inuvik.

Once stationed at their first posting, these young officers no longer live the stringent military existence of training depot and no matter how healthy their life style, they put on a few pounds. So at the moment, Constable Jackson Pedley's most serious concern was whether his Red Serge still fit! He patted his stomach as he went into his bedroom to collect the Sam Browne belt, lanyard, Stetson hat and all the other gear required to 'don the Serge'.

Meanwhile, as Pedley worried about his special guests arriving by RCMP plane in a few hours, Brian and his crew were awaiting the reaction from Boulder and the imminent impending doom that was sure to follow.

Chapter Nine

C onstable Jackson Pedley stood at attention on the Everet Airport tarmac as the RCMP twin otter taxied up beside him. He was definitely going to freeze to death at these temperatures. He tried not to think about his ten toes cramped into his polished leather High-Browns and the numbness already setting in, as the contingent stepped out of the plane and negotiated the short but slippery staircase to ground level.

Pedley had never met any Japanese officials before and he was not prepared in the least for their definition of casual dress. The five middle-aged men had obviously shopped very carefully for their northern attire. Each man wore a variation of a tartan flannel shirt and spanking new, very navy, blue jeans, neatly pressed and pulled up to the waist. Their designer belts looked ridiculously out of place with the jeans. The parkas were even more bizarre. One man wore a Hudson Bay blanket coat. It was ivory wool with the classic, wide red, green and yellow horizontal stripes. Jackson had not seen one of those coats before, except in his grade school history books. Two others had on Eastern Arctic Inuit parkas and the remaining two were wearing some sort of Russian fur coat, both of which were dragging on the ground, since the average height of all five men was about five foot two inches. They were each wearing elaborate mukluks that must have been given to them as gifts upon arrival. Mukluks are traditional footwear for indigenous peoples of the north. A lot of northern residents still wore the footwear, made from home-tanned moose-hide and a special northern wool, but the variation for everyday wear were called work mukluks and were very plain and practical. These men were wearing dress mukluks covered in satin embroidery and sparkling beadwork. For a fleeting moment, Jackson thought he had been set up by the Whitehorse office and that this was some kind of elaborate practical joke, but no, even his fellow Mounties would not go to this expense for a laugh. These were truly Japanese officials and he was going to accompany this odd group of costumed guests around town.

Pedley saluted the group and they in turn each bowed deeply to him. "On behalf of the Government of Canada and the Royal Canadian Mounted Police, I would like to welcome you to the Yukon, and the town of Everet. I hope that you find your short time here interesting and informative," said Jackson.

There were replies in unison from the group, none of which Jackson understood, since it was all in Japanese, and an overabundance of smiling, bowing and back-slapping. Finally one of the men spoke. "It is a great honour to be here. I am sorry, but they do not speak English. Do you speak Japanese?" he asked.

"Oh sure, I picked it up in Edmonton last summer!" thought Jackson, but he smiled and said, "No, I'm sorry I don't."

"Wakari mashita, I understand," replied the only English speaker. "We shall traverse this great country of yours and learn from our extraordinary visions of nature rather than the spoken word of our honourable and most esteemed guide."

The statement had obviously been memorized by the man, because when Jackson continued with "Well let's head off to town then," all five men stood still, smiling and nodding at him and each other, as if he was still giving his welcome speech. So he motioned to his truck and began to walk toward it, which gave the guests the necessary clue and they followed in a chatty cluster with murmurs of 'hai, hai' and strange vocal sounds that Jackson had never heard before.

This was going to be an experience and a half, Jackson thought, as he practically lifted each short man into his huge RCMP crew cab truck and swung the vehicle around and headed off to town.

Now three o'clock on a Sunday afternoon should have been a quiet time in Everet. People were usually recovering from Saturday night, or preparing for another week of work. It was the unofficial nap time for most of the adults, so Jackson was quite sure that if all went well, this tour of his would be over and done with, and the guests placed back on the plane before anyone in town even knew that there had been visitors. Unfortunately for Constable Pedley and his international contingent, an ad hoc community watch group had been appointed, and was on duty, patrolling the town and awaiting whatever action the town of Boulder was preparing to implement. Jackson had no idea that his quiet little community had turned into a fortress, with security in place that would equal a United Nations Peacekeeping Force.

The airport was seven kilometres north of town, just off the Alaskan highway, the only road in or out of Everet. The RCMP truck was about two kilometres from town when Jackson rounded a curve and came upon four trucks parked sideways across the highway and blocking the road completely. He recognized Brian and Eddie, and the other men as Everet residents. "What on earth is this?" he mumbled to himself. He smiled at his guests and they all nodded and smiled back, as he stopped his truck and got out to talk with Brian.

"What the hell is going on?" asked Pedley.

"Nothing to worry about," answered Brian, "We've just put a few preventative measures in place as a result of a little joke that we played on Boulder last night."

"No! No! Not today! Oh God, what have you assholes done now?" moaned Jackson.

"Nothing undeserved, and really quite funny and creative," smiled Brian.

"Am I laughing?" yelled Jackson.

"Listen, you obviously have some sort of official business at hand, and honestly, all this road block does is ensure that the town is nice and quiet for your visitors," Brian was trying to soothe Pedley and discourage him from asking for more details. "How long are they in town?"

"Just two hours. Can you idiots keep things normal for two hours?" Jackson said through clenched teeth.

"Of course! Go! Enjoy! Everything is under control here," said Eddie.

Pedley glared at both men before walking back to his vehicle and putting it into gear. One of the trucks moved to the side of the road to allow the RCMP truck to pass and then reversed itself back into road block position. Jackson would have to deal with this later. Right now he had five smiling, nodding Japanese men dressed like something from a 1920 North Pole expedition to entertain for two hours.

Chapter Ten

"The town looks pretty normal," thought Jackson with relief. He drove the men around showing them the small cottage hospital, the grocery store, the RCMP office and the gas station. That took about ten minutes and Jackson was worried about how to stretch this tour into two hours. Then he thought of the small sawmill near the school. He remembered talking with the owner of the mill a few months earlier and asking him how business was going. The owner had told him that business was very good because he had a new contract for logs with a Japanese company. Apparently the Japanese were fascinated with log cabins and the sawmill owner was gambling that this may be a burgeoning market and had invested heavily in developing contacts in Osaka. Obviously the manager was correct, because upon arrival at the mill, all five men struggled out of the truck and then were off in a flash. They were taking snapshots of everything and meticulously studying the timber piled around the yard. The Hudson Bay blanket fellow was even measuring the two-by-fours and recording the results on paper. The two men in the Russian fur coats were measuring the diameter of the prepped logs and closely studying the wood grains and the growth rings on each log end. They gathered chips from various piles and placed them in a small bag. Each man smelled everything. They smelled the wood, they smelled the chips, they smelled the sawdust and every few minutes each would stand still and take in a very deep breath and exhale slowly through clenched teeth. There were numerous nods of agreement and deep conversation. It was all very serious and scientific.

They talked with each other the entire time, obviously discussing the wood type, the measurements of the pieces piled near each saw, the equipment used and the manufacturer labels. This had definitely been a good idea, smiled Pedley, they had already been here an hour. While the men continued their studies, Jackson went into the mill office. He had a key to most businesses in town for security reasons. He grabbed a pile of business cards and went back out to his guests. If the Japanese government was so interested in spruce, he may as well try to put Everet on the maps in Tokyo. He gave each of them a few cards and they seemed to understand. They bowed almost in reverence and studied the cards for a long time while nodding and taking in large breathes of air through clenched teeth. Odd, thought Jackson, I guess they can read English albeit rather slowly! Jackson did not know that the exchanging of business cards was a formal and very important procedure in Japan.

When Jackson finally lifted each man back into the truck, there was only thirty minutes left, before he needed to return them to the airport, for their flight to Whitehorse. His final stop was the Everet Inn. He parked at the far end of the lot so everyone would not be watching as he struggled to lift the guests out of the cab again.

He had the group back on terra firma and they were walking toward the inn when it happened, swiftly and unexpectedly. They heard the noise first. Then suddenly the noise was so loud that two of the visitors covered their ears. Snowmobiles descended on the parking lot from every direction. Jackson estimated at least one hundred machines all swerving and circling the hotel parking lot at random. The noise of so many machines was deafening. It was still very sunny and he squinted to try and pick out some faces. Most of the men were wearing balaclavas. Woollen knit winter hats that covered the head completely with only openings for the eyes, nose and mouth. They were needed when driving snowmobiles in these temperatures. The wind chill temperature can be twenty degrees lower than the actual 'standing still' temperatures. A few of the men had pulled up their balaclavas as their machines slowed down and it was then that he recognized a couple of drivers. These were Boulder men surrounding the most important building in town. "Oh God please don't let them take my guests as hostages!" prayed Pedley.

Everything happened so fast that Constable Pedley did not have any time to worry much about any potential hostage crisis. Most of the machines had only one driver and just kept circling and distracting everyone, while twenty snowmobiles had two men on each, a driver and a passenger sitting behind. The machines that were carrying two men pulled up to various locations and the passengers jumped off while their drivers sped off to continue driving around and intimidating pedestrians. Things were happening at such a pace that Everet residents were just standing and staring in shocked disbelief. Within five minutes, the flag flying high above the hotel had been drawn down and replaced with the flag of Japan. The hotel sign high on the roof had been covered with a new sign reading 'Don't stop here, go on to Boulder'. Eddie's gas station had a new sign that read 'Closed Permanently'. They strung lengths of those plastic coloured flags that car lots use as decoration all around the town, each flag stamped clearly with 'Boulder'. It looked like a circus ground rather than a small town. When all the men were back on the snowmobiles they fell into one line, made a final circle around the hotel parking lot surrounding Jackson and his guests, and then stopped. The drivers of some of the machines lifted their seats and reached into the storage area of their machine. Each man lifted out a curling stone, turned to face the centre of the circle, and then each delivered their granite stone smoothly and strongly toward Jackson and his five Japanese businessmen. As these curling stones were all gliding in to meet each other, the snowmobiles careened off into the bush and disappeared.

There stood Jackson Pedley in the middle of the parking lot, with his five oddly dressed little visitors, surrounded by twenty curling stones that had all stopped within ten feet of the group. With the snowmobiles gone, the silence was deafening but it lasted only a moment, because suddenly the Japanese officials were applauding and bowing and slapping Jackson on his back with such exuberance that the young officer was truly confused and disoriented.

"Well that took care of the last twenty minutes of the tour," smiled Jackson, as he lifted his guests into his truck for the last time. And for some bizarre reason they seemed to actually enjoy the attack. "I don't care," Jackson said to himself, "I just have to get these guys out of this loony bin and back on the plane before anything else happens!" He drove as quickly as he could toward the airport. At the Everet checkpoint two miles out of town, he slowed down as the men let him through their pickup truck barrier and he yelled out the window, "Your road blocks really did the trick gentlemen. I just met about one hundred guys from Boulder at the hotel!"

"What?" screamed Brian and they all piled into their trucks and sped off in the other direction towards town.

Jackson said his farewells at the plane, which seemed to go on forever, until finally all the Japanese guests were on board and the pilot was able to close the door. He stood at attention once more and saluted the plane as it taxied away with each of the five guests nodding, smiling and waving from their windows. When the plane was air bound, he turned and limped toward his vehicle. These damn High-Browns! His feet were killing him!

Chapter Eleven

"We've been had gentlemen!" announced Brian to his troops in the hotel bar, "but I must say, we've been had by the best. This is the most elaborate payback I've seen in years." He was standing in the centre of the room and he turned slowly, his beer bottle raised above his head as he said, "To Boulder, may they not rest in peace, nor get another good night's sleep while they worry about the future of their town and the plans being made in Everet!"

"To Boulder!" everyone said in unison. The only two missing were Bob and Eddie who were both busy removing the temporary signs from their buildings. Neither of the men could relax until the 'go on to Boulder' and 'permanently closed' banners were removed. They were removing them carefully and hanging them in the garage to dry. Such items were valuable and must be preserved carefully for the future. It was absolutely normal to keep odd regalia in the community arsenal as they could be used again for events yet unforeseen. Recycling was in place in these northern communities long before it became fashionable in the south.

"This is truly an historical moment. Brian paying tribute to the men of Boulder," Mary leaned back in her chair and looked up at the tavern ceiling.

"There is nothing finer, than the feeling of joy one experiences, knowing that the enemy is up to our challenge. It is a proud man who knows his enemies are intelligent and worthy of respect," Brian said with mock formality.

"How did they know we had roadblocks?" someone asked.

"I don't think they even thought of roadblocks. I think the problem was that we never thought of snowmobiles," contemplated Father O'Reilly.

"It was absolutely fantastic!" said Mary. "It looked like some sort of bizarre Shriners' Convention, but they had snowmobiles rather than those mini motorbikes."

"And balaclavas, rather than those red Fez!" noted Sandra.

Father O'Reilly stood up at the mention of his Protestant nemeses. "Those damn Shriners! They circled the Pro-Cathedral last time they had a convention in my home town. They wouldn't leave until the Knights of Columbus gathered and ran them off with their swords." He laughed thinking about it. Grown men in red Fez and others in purple robes all chasing each other around a cathedral! A good time was had by all. If only Northern Ireland could reach that stage of acceptance.

"Well it sure is fun to spar with worthy opponents," said Brian, "There's nothing more boring than playing a practical joke on someone who has no sense of the importance of retribution."

"I hope they're saying the same about us," added Mary.

"We know they are. They wouldn't have planned such a spectacular show today, if they hadn't been thoroughly impressed and pissed off with our 'Upside Down Road Sign Campaign'!" noted Brian.

"True, true," everyone murmured proudly.

"You know the funniest part?" continued Mary. "Jackson Pedley, standing in the middle of the parking lot, with those five strange looking little men, and curling stones coming at them from all directions!" She could hardly speak through her chortling.

"Yea, what the hell was that all about?" sputtered Brian. Now everyone was flying high again, and through it all only short comments could be uttered through the gasps for breath. With every phrase that someone managed to say, the wave would surge again. "Red Serge", "Hudson Bay blanket coat", "Dr. Zivago", "He had to lift them into the truck".

It was then that Pedley walked into the bar. He had gone back home and peeled off his Red

Serge and brown riding boots, had a hot shower and changed into his more comfortable blue jeans and regular uniform shirt before coming back to the centre of town to see everyone.

"Pedley! I hope we haven't caused some kind of international crisis!" shouted Brian.

"Tell me, would you really care if you had?" Jackson replied with a friendly glare.

Brian pretended to think for a moment then said, "No!" and the whole room was filled with boisterous merriment again.

"I didn't think so," Jackson said, rolling his eyes.

"Who were those guys?" asked Bob who was back from restoring his hotel sign.

"Some group of Japanese government officials," answered Jackson.

"Japanese!" gasped Mary. "The Boulder idiots raised a flag of Japan over the hotel."

"That's right! Oh God, why me? Why a flag of Japan?" groaned Pedley.

"I know why the flag," said Eddie, "one of them won it from me in a poker game last summer. I can't remember where I got it. I think it was from some high school project years ago." The bantering rose again.

Sandra had to go and bring a couple of boxes of Kleenex into the bar. There was so much laughter and so many tears created, everyone's sleeves were damp from wiping their eyes. Brian looked around the room with a nostalgic, sentimental smile. He put his arm around

Mary, "It doesn't get any better than this, does it Babe?"

"Yes it's wonderful," thought Mary, but she was also thinking that it can wear a little thin. "Wasn't there more to life than moments like these? I think I love this man and I know I love the fun we have together, but are we building a future? He works hard, but he never talks about work. It's like some peripheral thing he does only to support the parties and the good times. It's that damn Protestant work ethic kicking in again, Mary. God rewards hard work."

Her family were great socialisers, but they also could work fourteen hours a day, seven days a week when duty called. No type of labour was below them and no function above them. "I'm so bourgeoisie! But it's who I am. Gotta build on the family wealth. Gotta leave the next generation a little better off than the last. That damn King James Version of the Bible. What a great political tool that was. Kept the throngs working through the Industrial Revolution and it's still haunting me." She turned back from her thoughts and studied Brian's face. "I don't know. I just don't know."

Bob stood up and raised his glass, "To life, laughter and friends, and to Brian for having the energy and fortitude to have us fight back!" he paused through murmurs of 'Here, here!', then he continued, "And . . . to the Queen!" At that, everyone stood up and took a sip. Bob leaned down to the only person sitting, "Sorry Father!"

Just then one of the staff members hollered into the room, "Phone call for Constable Pedley!"

Jackson rose and went into the lobby. The receptionist told him to use the line in Bob's office. He was standing as he answered the phone with his usual 'Constable Pedley here'. It was Ottawa! Oh God! The Japanese guys were only in Whitehorse, and already Ottawa had heard. The colour drained from Jackson's face and he fell into Bob's chair as the person on the other end began to speak.

"Constable Jackson Pedley," the voice had said, "Please hold for the Commissioner." The Commissioner! Jackson's head was reeling. He could hear it already. We station you in the one of the smallest postings in the nation and you still manage to create international havoc. I'm sorry you're assigned to foot patrol on the DEW line; maybe there you can stay out of trouble for the rest of your career! The young officer was miserable. He had never felt more ashamed or incompetent. What RCMP officer could not handle a brief tour of an area? Two hours is about as short as it gets. He was given a simple, small task and had let down his entire organization. He was still admonishing himself when a voice came back on the telephone line. "Constable Pedley?"

"Yes sir." answered the now shaking and perspiring Jackson.

"Commissioner here. Young man, I don't pretend to understand the workings of the north completely. I was stationed in the Eastern Arctic briefly thirty years ago, but I've been told the Northwest is quite different and yet somehow the same. Regardless, your actions today may well be the most extraordinary and impressive show of just what this force can accomplish as we enter this modern era of international trade and cooperation."

"Yes sir," Jackson was still shaking and perspiring, but now he sat up a little straighter in the chair and listened more closely. He had only been half listening and he still was not sure if he was being reprimanded or congratulated.

"I don't know how you pulled this event together with just two hours notice, but it puts our national planning committee here in Ottawa to shame. Lumber displays, synchronized snowmobile parade, security systems on the highway and Constable, raising the Japanese flag in the centre of town was a real coup de grâce! The Japanese contingent said it was the most amazing welcome they have received since their visit began. They said the use of such a large team of snowmobiles, working in unison, paid sublime tribute to the Japanese culture's fundamental philosophy of society working in unison for the betterment of all. They feel that with this important similarity between our two countries it is only natural we begin serious trade talks and work to create joint ventures. My Lord son, you're a one-man diplomatic team! I just wanted to tell you personally that your performance today will be recorded and the Canadian Government and The Force appreciate your effort on our behalf. Keep up the good work Constable Pedley and sleep well tonight knowing that you have performed above and beyond the call of duty."

"Thank you sir!" answered Jackson as the phone line went dead. He hung up the receiver and leaned back in the chair. "Thank you God," thought Pedley. "They loved it! I don't understand any of it. I don't understand what was going on in town today. I don't understand how they planned it all. And I really don't understand why no one was injured with a curling stone! And what are the odds of a Japanese flag being hoisted at that moment, in that place?" He smiled to himself and thought about Everet more. "They just let me pretend that I'm controlling some aspect of this community. This town runs any which way it chooses. I'm just standing on the sidelines watching a movie. I may as well start buying popcorn and enjoying it! Yes man, just go with the flow and stop trying to swim upstream," he chuckled as he got up to join the others in the bar.

III

Miracles and Long Winter
Nights

Chapter Twelve

Everet was quiet leading up to Christmas. December 25th was a little different in the north. There were no stores, except the food outlet, to decorate. It was too cold to put up lights on the streets. Some people strung one or two string of lights on their houses, but the cost of electricity prohibited any elaborately lit up houses.

Almost every job in town would be considered essential services, so no one really took many days off. The only people to actually have substantial and complete holidays were the teachers, as the school did officially shut down for the Christmas season. Every other business tried to run with shorter shifts or employees on call. So on the morning of December 23rd Mary was enjoying her first cup of tea and sitting in her pyjamas, as Brian was getting dressed for work and gobbling down some breakfast.

"Something's been haunting me Babe and I wanted to talk with you about it," said Brian.

"What is it?" asked Mary.

"It's this. You know Brad Kincaid, the new guy in town that we hired part time to help us out when we need more hands?" asked Brian.

Mary nodded, "He's married and has two little girls, doesn't he?"

"That's right. He's a hard worker, but an odd sort of guy, you know, a loner type. He's quiet and keeps to himself. They're living out of town in one of those tiny little cabins near the airport. It's warm enough. I know that because he made a deal with Jim for wages and propane for the cabin's tanks. But they have nothing Mary. And I know those kids aren't getting any gifts or visits from Santa this year. I don't know how old they are, but they both look about five years old. That's a magic year Mary! That's when you really believe. I mean really and honestly believe . . . in fairies and goblins and Santa. Remember the feelings of really believing hon?"

"Yea, I do," replied Mary and her eyes began to cloud with moisture. Then she shook herself out of the moment and continued, "But you don't have to remember, because you still do believe in fairies and goblins and Santa!"

"You're damn right! 'Cause they're real! Think about it. Parents all over the western world secretly buy presents for their children. There are no handbooks or courses, just this massive, wonderful secret. Who could coordinate such an elaborate charade? It's more of a miracle than the actual Santa façade. No one breaks the code, except the odd, bitter cynic who had Christmas ruined for him so he ruins it for his kids," he started singing as he brought his empty coffee cup to the sink. "Oh you better watch out, you better not cry, you better not pout, I'm telling you why . . . Santa Claus is coming to town!"

Mary was still in a serious mood. "Why is it that some people always live on the fringes of society?" she pondered. "They never join a community or make friends."

"I don't know; past lives, secrets, mistakes, insecurities, or bitterness. Whatever the reason it's sure to be a sad one," said Brian. "You know life is like a pond, and if you're lucky then you can be a very special pebble."

"What the heck are you talking about?" Mary asked with a mystified look.

"Wait, wait, I digress!" Brian loved throwing formal words into casual conversation, "This family is broke and it's Christmas. How often do we ever get a chance to truly give? I mean in the real sense of the word; anonymously, with no one ever knowing about your actions except you and maybe your partner." He winked and smiled at Mary. "Let's buy the girls Christmas presents and quietly leave them at the door of the cabin on Christmas Eve."

"Brian that's fantastic! Good idea," said Mary, "but we'll have to work fast.

"I know, and that's why it has to be a team effort. One, I have to work today and tomorrow, and two, I don't know what to buy little girls unless I was in a store and could look at everything. Even then I'd probably screw up."

"Okay leave it with me," said Mary, "I'll call the department store in Whitehorse and order everything and you find some trucker going south, to pick up the boxes at the shop this afternoon and drop them off here sometime before tomorrow night. I'll make sure everything is ready at the shop by noon today."

"What a team! What a team! You're a beautiful lady," Brian kissed her on her forehead, then one cheek, then the other.

"Yes, and you're a sentimental ham," she kissed him back.

"Love ya, Babe," he hollered as he raced to his truck which had been warming up in the driveway.

"Me too," smiled Mary as she went back to pour another cup of tea and call Whitehorse.

Mary telephoned the only department store in Whitehorse and asked to speak with the owner. She would have to make special arrangements for payment. When she was transferred to his line, she explained who she was and was fortunate because she had met him at a tourist conference a few months earlier and he remembered meeting her. She explained that she wanted to purchase some toys for a couple of really needy children and could she mail him a cheque. She was lucky. He was a nice man anyway, but it was also Christmas and that usually puts almost everyone into a more generous and benevolent mood. He agreed to the arrangements and even offered her special assistance from his daughter who was home from university and helping him out with the holiday rush.

The store owner's daughter literally walked the aisles and described to Mary every item still available. Together they chose two magnificent dolls because they had agreed that every little girl needs a new doll at Christmas. Next they picked out a tea set, a little wooden table with two chairs, cradles for the new dolls, and then two lovely stockings and various little items to fill each one. They also both agreed that every child needs new Christmas nightwear and there were two beautiful red nightgowns still on a shelf. Mary was really enjoying the '70s version of virtual shopping and was just finishing up with the details for the pick up when the daughter gasped and hesitated for a moment. She explained that she did not want to ruin all of their hard work but she had just spied the ultimate gift in the store. She described it to Mary as best she could. It was a wooden doll-house with ten rooms. Each room was furnished with sturdy wooden furniture and all had been hand painted, and each room had curtains, and dishes, vases and bedding. There was a family of four including Mother, Father and two little girls. The original family included a little boy but he had been damaged in transit. They'd had a giggle over that and agreed that most men were often 'damaged in transit'. Neither of them knew exactly what it meant, but it sounded funny at the time. Mary could envision every detail of the dollhouse. When she asked the all important question, the shopkeeper's daughter gave her a price that equalled the price of the other entire package of items. Mary wavered for a few seconds and then said, "What the hell! It's Christmas! I'll take it!" The girl promised to have everything packed up and ready for the unnamed trucker that would be in by noon to pick up and deliver the boxes. Mary hung up the phone and smiled. Brian was right. It feels really good to give!

Since Mary was on holidays, Brian came home for lunch. He was kicking off his boots when Mary approached with a hug.

He told her that he had found a driver to stop by the store in Whitehorse, pay the shop for their order and pick everything up before one o'clock. They could then grab the stuff from him on his way through Everet and pay him back for the purchase. He also explained that the driver was trying to get home for Christmas morning and would still have eight hundred miles to drive by the time he hit Everet. If he drove all night he could be home sometime Christmas morning.

"Poor guy! That's really kind of him to take the time to stop for us, and even pay for it," said Mary.

"Well it's funny how the world works Mary. This is kind of a win-win situation. He needs a favour from us. You see, he has three sons, eleven, nine and six years old. He just got paid in Anchorage for his last haul, so he has all this cash and his wife only has a little. She's bought a few little Santa things but that's it. He needs stuff for his boys."

Mary laughed. "The shop in Whitehorse is going to think I'm Howard Hughes when I phone back for another order!"

So Brian went back to work and Mary called the shop again and asked for the daughter she had been speaking with earlier. She explained the story to the woman and off they went again on a shopping spree. Mary was quite proud of their team work since this involved more than toys. They agreed that gifts from parents should include clothing, and perhaps for the older boys, more significant things like globes or interesting books. The daughter even offered to wrap the boys' gifts when she heard how this hardworking trucker was trying to bring home the bacon and be such a good parent. It brought tears to Mary's eyes. She was envisioning this lonely, tired work- ing man, wanting to give his family a special Christmas while driving through an isolated and barren landscape, and the miracle of a season that brings out the best in everyone who was helping him do it.

Mary was really feeling the Christmas spirit by the time she finished the second phone call and poured herself a tall rye and ginger as a reward. Canadians drink rye whisky. There are various whiskies on earth, but the average Canadian knows of only one blend that satisfies the palate and that is the whisky made from rye. All whiskies begin with a grain. The word whisky originates from the Gaelic word for water. The Scots and Irish often use a longer phrase which means water of life. Scotland has been producing Scotch whisky for hundreds of years with a base from barley. The Americans make a whisky from corn maize, but they call it Bourbon. To be called a Whisky on the label, it usually originates in Scotland, Ireland, Canada or Japan since the processes follows stringent rules, some legal and some simply accepted traditional protocol.

Mary was curled up with a book and on her second rye and ginger when Brian called and told her to meet him in half an hour for his coffee break at the hotel. She ran out to start her truck and let it warm up. Nothing could be done spontaneously in these temperatures!

When she arrived at the hotel coffee shop, Brian was already sitting there with Eddie who had a large suitcase sitting beside him. She sat down beside Brian and asked Eddie where on earth he was going at three in the afternoon on the day before Christmas Eve.

Brian answered for him. "Well Babe, as luck would have it, Eddie mentioned to me at the shop today that he was sorry he hadn't planned better for the holidays. His wife's gone off to Toronto to visit her side of the family. He's sitting here all alone. His sister isn't well and he would really like to visit with her, but he doesn't want to drive all the way out to Alberta and then have to dread the drive back up here. There are no more flights till next week. When I told him about the great trucker who is helping us out, he felt sorry for him."

"Yea," said Eddie, "It's too bloody dangerous to try and drive straight through the eight hundred miles without any sleep! He's already been awake and driving for at least twelve hours. If I go with him, I can share the driving, he gets there in time and alive, and I can see my sister and fly back in next week."

"It's perfect!" said Mary, "You're perfect!" she smiled at Brian.

"I know, I know. God gave me these impeccable organizational skills. It would be a sin to waste them," he said smugly.

"And so humble," laughed Eddie.

"Okay skills at work again!" said Brian. "The guy called me from the toy shop at twelve. He had everything and left Whitehorse a little after noon. It's three thirty now, he'll be here about five o'clock. He's going to make a quick stop at TranGas. I'll pay him. Eddie will jump in and drive. All is well!"

"About the payment, Babe," Mary grimaced.

"No problem Mary! I stopped at the bank on my way back to work after lunch," said Brian.

"It's closed now, isn't it?" asked Mary.

"How much did you spend?" asked Brian.

"Well, I suspect a little more than you budgeted," murmured Mary.

"How much more, oh love of my life and keeper of our savings?" whispered Brian.

Mary spit it out, "About twice as much as originally discussed."

"On that note, I'm off to the can," smiled Eddie and he trotted off to the washroom.

Mary thought Brian would have been furious, but this man never ceased to amaze her. Not only did he take it in his stride, and with enormous pleasure, but he continued by telling her that he had stopped off at the grocery store and bought two weeks worth of food for the family of four.

"Don't worry, if I don't have enough, I can borrow from the till and repay Jim after the holidays." Brian took her in his arms, "Sweetheart, I have an old adage about giving, if it doesn't hurt to write the cheque then it isn't enough!"

"We'll never get rich this way!" said Mary.

Brian whispered in her ear, "It depends on how you count your riches, my lovely!"

Chapter Thirteen

*T*he drop off and repayment were completed without a hitch. The trucker was thrilled to have Eddie accompany him. He thanked Mary profusely for all her help, wiping a few tears from his cheeks as he said how happy his boys and his wife would be. He told them that the shop-keeper's daughter had even taken the initiative to purchase a gold nugget watch for his wife. She had assured him that the jeweller had promised her that she could return it if he didn't want it.

"Didn't want it, I replied, I'm gonna look like a goddamn saint tomorrow morning!" the trucker had smiled as he repeated his words for Brian, Eddie and Mary.

So with the two men and the transport trailer off and heading south, Brian and Mary secured all the gifts and food in the back of her truck. Brian locked up the office and they drove back home separately.

Jackson's truck was in the driveway when they got home. He and Father O'Reilly were stopping for a bit of Christmas cheer. They settled in the living room. Mary had even bought a bottle of Scotch so the priest could have his favourite 'water of life'. Everyone had a drink and Mary was in the kitchen preparing some special snacks. She could hear Brian's voice. He was telling them how Eddie had decided to drive south with the truck driver.

"By God those men work hard!" he was saying, "I don't care what you say, a freight train can hold a lot of shit, but it's the trucks and their drivers that are the backbone of this nation. Damn those men are strong. They're hardly ever home, they work long hours, and they spend most of their waking hours worried about the next truck payment."

"Those trucks cost as much as a house and you always have to have contingency plans for repairs," added Jackson.

"And don't forget the tires," continued Father O'Reilly, "It costs a small fortune in rubber every year."

"Not to mention changing the darn things in sub-zero temperatures or in the mud and muck of the spring," said Mary as she entered the room carrying her tray of holiday delights.

"This looks delicious Mary!" said the priest, "You must have a little bit of Irish blood in you."

"I'm Canadian Father," she laughed, "I imagine I have a little bit of every nationality in me!"

"Well there is something to say for you mutts!" said the Irishman.

They all laughed and toasted the coming Christmas Eve.

The next morning followed the same routine as the previous day, except this time there were no chores to be discussed. Brian and Mary had bought each other their gifts weeks ago and they were wrapped and under the tree. They had also sent off presents to their families a month earlier and had gifts from both families sitting in colourful piles. The kitchen was full of food and drink. The only thing they had to discuss was the drop off at the small cabin sometime later in the day. Brian had covered the box of Mary's truck with a heavy tarp to protect everything in case it snowed. The only thing they had brought into the house were the fresh vegetables, so they wouldn't freeze, but Brian had also shopped wisely and purchased mostly frozen and canned goods, so they would last longer. When money is tight, fresh food is a luxury he had told Mary.

"Let's leave about dusk," Brian had suggested.

"Well that narrows it down to anytime between one and seven o'clock," laughed Mary.

"I'm using the term in the traditional manner, my dear," said Brian, lifting his head in a mock version of snobbish rebuff. "I'm referring to some time in the early evening."

"Gotcha!" replied Mary. "Okay then, about six o'clock should be good. I hope we can pull this off without being seen."

"It's Christmas; the time of miracles!" Brian smiled, putting on his heavy winter work boots and stepping out once more into the freezing Arctic air.

"Miracles!" repeated Mary as she sat at the kitchen table with her thumb at her lips. She rested her chin on her right hand and stared at the wall. "Miracles." she said again, except this time more sadly and quietly. She sat there for some time contemplating the word and the season.

Mary's family were Christian, and Christmas was an important event in their home, as it was in millions of other homes around the world. They had attended church regularly and supported all the annual events of the parish. She and Brian had both been raised in the United Church of Canada.

When the early immigrants arrived in the new world, the numbers had been small, especially in the northern realms of the Dominion of Canada. There were people of all denominations. Of course there were lots of Roman Catholics between the French and the Irish settlers, and due to the fact that the Roman Catholic Church, being the original large Christian group, had kept a large number intact during the Reformation five hundred years earlier. But the 'protestors' or Protestants had splintered off into innumerable factions, and so with the early Roman Catholic settlers, also came the Anglicans, Lutherans, Presbyterians, Congregationalists, Methodists and Episcopalians.

Initially, Canada had a miniscule population and some of the Protestant groups were too small to form large congregations and build separate churches. In 1925 The United Church of Canada was formed when the Methodist Church of Canada, the Congregational Union of Canada, and seventy per cent of the Presbyterian Church in Canada, as well as the small General Council of Union Churches in the west, entered into a union. In retrospect it was an amazing achievement. Four groups with long and varied religious traditions and nationalities overlooked their differences to join together, albeit out of necessity, to rejoice in their similarities. With such a dynamic beginning, it is no wonder that Mary and Brian found themselves raised within a community of empathy, political tolerance and astounding liberal attitudes towards their spiritualism and faith.

With this United Church background, Mary and Brian's Sunday school classes did not spend much time glorifying mystery, but rather explaining the miracles and mysteries. The Red Sea had not opened miraculously for the Israelites, but rather they had managed to struggle through the swamps at low tide, whereas the Egyptians with their heavy armour and horses had simply sunk as the tide came back in. Bread did not fall from heaven in the desert; rather flocks of migrating

birds often died and fell to the ground during particularly dry seasons.

Mary had been raised with a tacit understanding that miracles were far deeper and less
tangible than those of an omnipotent illusion-
ist. Miracles were about human healing, human
strength and fortitude, human kindness and love,
and today she and Brian were going to exemplify
that kind of miracle. Two people had taken the
time, and initiated an act of kindness for which
no one would ever give them credit. There would
be no thank you and no platitudes, just the enormous satisfaction and personal joy they would
experience once the plan had been completed.
"Now that's a miracle!" Mary told herself, "And
Brian is even more selfless because he noticed
the family and recognized their need. Why didn't
I notice that family?" she contemplated. "He is
truly a man of good will."

She spent the rest of the day making special dips and traditional hors d'oeuvres to enjoy
over the next few days. Mary did not like cooking very much but she loved making appetizers.
Brian called her the Queen of Hors d'Oeuvres
and said he rather liked the menus. "Makes me
feel that I'm at a never ending cocktail party," he
would tease her.

Brian arrived home promptly at five and had
a quick shower. Mary was waiting for him and
already had the remaining fresh food at the front
door. Brian was so excited and wound up for the

secret drop off that he did not even bother to dry his hair.

They hopped into Mary's truck and were off. As they drove through town they could not believe their luck. Sitting in front of the hotel was Brad Kincaid's old green truck. Mary ran into the hotel to pretend she was using the washroom, ran back out to announce that the entire family was inside having a coffee. Brian raced over to their truck, turned it off and removed a spark plug. They sped off to the cabin.

The door to the cabin was unlocked. Nobody locked their doors in Everet. Obviously the crime rate was low, but it also came from a long northern tradition that provided safety and warmth to anyone passing by. It would be a sad thing to find a person frozen at your front door because the entrance had been locked.

Both Mary and Brian rushed to bring everything into the cabin. They had time to pull everything out of the boxes. Brian put all the gifts in one corner of the cabin; there was no tree. Mary put all the food in the fridge or on the table. They hardly had any time to enjoy the scene, but they took a few seconds at the door to look back and view the room. It looked spectacular.

They closed the cabin door and stood on the path for a few moments. The silence was deafening. Mary looked up at the clear night sky and the sparkling stars. Without thinking, she began to recite St. Luke. "And there were in the same country shepherds watching their flock. And behold an angel of the Lord stood by them, and the brightness of God shone round about them; and they feared with a great fear. And the angel said to them: Fear not; for, behold, I bring you good tidings of great joy that shall be to all the people: For unto you is born this day, in the city of David, a Saviour, who is Christ the Lord. And this shall be a sign unto you. You shall find the infant wrapped in swaddling clothes, and laying in a manger. And suddenly there was with the angel a multitude of the heavenly host, praising God, and saying: Glory to God in the highest; and on earth peace to men of good will."

"Amen! That's the clincher, isn't it?" Brian put his arm around Mary. "Peace to men of good will. The secret is to stop looking for peace and start trying to maintain good will."

Mary was looking at Brian. Calm had filled her eyes. Then she saw it. To the left of Brian's head, high on a spruce, sat the white owl. "Amazing," thought Mary, "Too amazing to even mention." She smiled and nodded to her Arctic angel, who twisted his neck and nodded back. The moment passed and reality set in. "Brian, you've got hoarfrost growing on your head!" Brian sauntered over to the truck and looked in the side mirror. "That's amazing, wish it would stay for the holidays. I look like a Christmas decoration!"

They put all the boxes back in Mary's truck and sped back to town. Mary drove back so Brian could hop out and replace the spark plug in Brad's truck and start it up again. Mary drove around to the rear of the hotel and dumped the boxes. The whole point of this exercise was to honestly dispose of any evidence that would link them to the deed.

When she drove back around to the front of the hotel, Brian was waiting for her by the parking lot lamp post. For a brief second Mary was reminded of the huge white snow owl she had been privileged to see for the first time, a month earlier, then Brian was inside the truck, giving her a huge hug and yelling "Tally ho!" as they swerved around and headed home.

Later that night, after numerous fancy drinks and appetizers, Brian and Mary lay in bed ready to cuddle up and doze off.

"What a great day, eh hon?" Brian whispered.

"Mmm-mmm," answered Mary.

"Remember when I told you about life being like a pond, and if you're lucky then you can be a very special pebble?"

"Mmmmmm," responded Mary.

"Well this is the kind of thing I mean. You're no heavy round stone, or one of the flat things that can jump across the water Mary Richardson. You're a very special pebble. Mary? Babe?"

Brian closed his eyes and snuggled in close to Mary who was already asleep.

Chapter Fourteen

Three weeks had passed since Christmas. The north was well into the depths of winter. Although December 21st is the shortest day of the year and after that the days begin to lengthen again, leading up to the longest day of the year which is June 21st; there is no anticipation of spring in mid-January. The first two months of the year are very long and cold, and they feel very dark and dreary. Perhaps it is the let down after the Christmas season, or the novelty of winter is simply dissipating, but most Canadians would choose one of these two months as their least favourite time of year. January and February are boring. Spring is a long way off and every day is either cold or colder.

Brian was sitting in his living room with Bob, Eddie and Jim. Mary and Jackson were over at the school running some kind of information evening for parents and students about the RCMP.

"I'm bored!" announced Brian.

"Join the club," answered Eddie, "Tires, tires, piston, and tires. That's my whole life these days."

Everyone grunted in agreement.

"Jackson is the only one having a good winter," Brian commented, "My God, how many plaques and letters of commendation has he received in the past month?"

"Two from the Mounties, one from the Prime Minister's office, one from the Lumberman's Association and even something from the Office of External Affairs!" Jim was listing them on his fingers.

"He's a goddamn national hero!" said Bob, who was also the postman, "I just delivered some crystal vase to him yesterday from Bombardier. Apparently the Japanese have just ordered thousands of snowmobiles."

They all burst out laughing at the memory of the 'attack of the Boulder skidoos' weeks earlier. The entire curling stone incident seemed like ancient history now. A cold northern week can feel like a month. The days feel like a week, and an hour just drags on into eternity.

"Well don't get me wrong, I love the guy," Brian was saying as he rose to get another beer, "but it's not fair. We did all the hard work for that whole scene. We triggered the event. If we hadn't frozen to death turning all those road signs upside down, none of it would have even happened."

"Yea, but we didn't do any of it to impress the Japanese, did we?" Bob commented.

"Neither did he!" answered Brian. "Pedley didn't know what the hell was going on! He was just in the right place at the right time."

"In his Red Serge with those five little guys dressed up for some foreign reproduction of *The Trail of '98*," laughed Jim.

"I know Robert Service wrote the story, but didn't they make a movie of it once?" asked Eddie.

"Yea, back in the twenties. I've never seen it. Don't like those oldies, but those Japanese guys were dressed up just the way I imagine men must have looked as they struggled over the mountains up to Dawson City," Jim continued. "Didn't you and Bob hike The Chilkoot?"

"Yea, two summers ago. It was nice, but I can't imagine walking it in the winter," said Brian.

"And not with a 'ton of gear' on your back!" added Bob.

"It's unbelievable what men can do when gold fever strikes. I guess if you've got nothing to lose, then anything is worth a try," Eddie said.

The Trail of '98 is the term given to the route used by thousands to reach Dawson City in 1898 when American newspapers started running stories of the gold found in the Yukon. It ran from a small settlement called Dyea, near Skagway, Alaska, directly over the mountains to Dawson City. Robert Service, a northern poet and writer, titled one of his works *The Trail of '98*. The actual route is called The Chilkoot

Trail and it runs thirty-three miles over the Coast Mountains. So many men came unprepared for such a hike, especially in winter, that the North-West Mounted Police who patrolled the Canadian portion of the trail insisted that each man bring a ton of provisions with him to ensure he could survive the initial phase of the adventure. It became known as the 'ton of gear'. Entrepreneurs carried amazing and outrageously heavy items over the trail, including pianos and cast iron stoves. The sad irony of the Trail of '98 is that the creek beds of the Yukon had already been worked and by the time word was out and tens of thousands left the depression in the United States to venture north and seek their fortune, most of the gold had already been extracted.

"You should see the interesting stuff left along the trail," said Brian. "Dishes, tools, stoves."

"There are even fifteen beds up top at the old North-West Mounted Police cabin at the border. Apparently the guy hauling them couldn't pay the tariff so he just left them and continued over to Dawson," explained Bob.

"It's like a thirty-three mile long museum," described Brian, "There aren't many trails that you hike to see what people have accomplished. Usually you go out hiking to get away from it all and enjoy nature, but this trail is more about people and history."

"Anyway, I can just picture some young policeman like Jackson, up top on the pass, collecting fees from five guys like the ones he was touring around six weeks ago!" laughed Bob.

They all chuckled again and then silence descended upon the group. Boredom is a heavy cloud to lift in mid-January, on a cold and dark evening.

"We've gotta do something to liven up this place," said Brian, "We need a plan!"

"You're the brains of this motley crew. Think of somethin'," Bob said as he took a swig of beer.

"Okay, okay," answered Brian, "First step is to choose the victim."

"Well it's too cold to look at Boulder yet. We need to save that for the spring. It's gotta be someone in town," Jim said.

"Father O'Reilly or Pedley then. We love them most!" suggested Bob.

"Yea, a good practical joke has got to be played on those you like," Brian philosophized, "Otherwise it's not a joke at all."

"How true!" said Jim, "I never thought of it that way before. If strangers had taken our curling stones, it would have been a theft, or just plain stupid. It's not a joke unless you know and like the victims."

"So who do we like more at the moment, the priest or the cop?" asked Eddie with a smile.

Bob thought for a moment, and then said, "I don't think it's a matter of choosing one over the other. We like them both. It's more a decision of who we think deserves our attention most at this particular moment in time."

They all looked at each other, nodded and said in unison, "Pedley!"

"Now the question is: what should we do to him?" smiled Brian with evil delight.

The ensuing discussion itself actually solved the boredom situation. The hours passed swiftly as they tossed ideas about and laughed about the consequences of each scenario. If no concrete plan had developed during the evening, no one would have been disappointed. The conversation had become much more interesting and the level of energy and enjoyment had more than doubled. But as with any gathering of creative and innovative minds, a plan did emerge. It was another one of those northern plans that only those who have experienced an isolated, cold winter in a place with no distractions like television or an actual downtown, can appreciate. It happens in a place where entertainment is not offered to the community, but rather a place where the community must create their own entertainment, and a new show was about to begin.

"We could do it tonight," said Eddie, "He's busy over at the school for at least another hour."

"No," said Brian, "Let's sit on it for a couple of days and make sure we have all the details well planned."

"Besides," Bob added, "Now that we have the idea, it'll make the week pass faster, if we have something to talk about."

"Truer words were never spoken!" said Jim, "I feel better than I've felt in weeks just thinking about it."

"This is the law of the Yukon, and ever she makes it plain: Send not your foolish and feeble; send me your strong and your sane," quoted Brian raising his glass high in a toast.

"And to the Queen!" added Eddie.

"That's no fun to say unless our Irish priest is around!" laughed Bob, "To Robert Service!"

"To Robert Service," they all repeated and took a drink.

Chapter Fifteen

The days passed quickly now that Brian had something to occupy his mind. Between work, secret meetings and phone calls from the other members of the plot club, life had become interesting and the weather much more bearable.

They had decided to wait until the end of January to carry out the plan. This way the first long month of the year could be spent enjoyably and the hardest part of the season would be over.

"You're up to something, aren't you?" asked Mary on the final Monday morning of January.

"What are you talking about?" replied Brian.

"Nobody is this perky in January. You haven't moaned or groaned once about the cold or the dark," she said as she continued the interrogation.

"Perky?" repeated Brian with a chuckle. "Who says 'perky'?"

Susan Bainbridge

"I say 'perky'! And that's what you are, friggin' perky!" she sneered. "Don't you be planning
anything that involves me. I'm in no mood for
humour at the moment."

"Aren't we pleasant this morning? Don't
worry, I save all my good plans for people who
will appreciate them. And you are clearly in no
mood this month to find the significant value, let
alone the subtle essence of my intelligence."

"Correct!" Mary put on her parka and opened
the front door. "Damn it's cold out there!" she
groaned as she closed the door and ran to her
truck.

Brian smiled to himself. Mary's mood just
emphasized how lucky he was to be feeling so
excited about the next few days. It was going
to be great! He pictured poor Pedley, sitting at
home polishing all his plaques and trophies. He
didn't know what was going to hit him. God he
had a good time teasing his officer friend. "Why
are some people so much fun to set up?" he wondered as he headed off to TranGas, "Because they
react so well to the trick and they can laugh at
themselves later." Jackson could do that. He was
a good sport.

They waited until a night when they knew that
Pedley would be out of the office. It was the last
Thursday of January and Jackson had gone up
to Whitehorse for a section meeting, so the men
could take their time as they carried out Operation Trupper. They pulled up to the police trailer
and went into the side room where the freezer

was kept. They opened the freezer and lifted out the frozen body of Johnny Michael.

"Jesus, shouldn't this place be more secure. The doors are unlocked, even the freezer isn't secured. Anybody could come in here and take a body," said Eddie.

"And tell me Eddie, who else besides us, would want to come in here and take a body for Christ's sake?" asked Brian.

Bob and Jim started laughing so hard that they doubled over and Johnny had to be put on the floor until they gained control of themselves. Brian smirked and said, "Okay team, get a grip! We laugh later. Let's get Johnny over to Jim's."

They picked up the corpse again, and put it into the back of Brian's truck. In twenty minutes, Johnny was resting soundly again in a new container. The freezer was a model they had been using in the showroom at TranGas, but a newer version had just arrived, so Jim had moved the older one to the work area in an adjoining building. They locked it up and Jim slipped the key into his office desk. Then they went over to the hotel to relish in their dirty deed.

"He's gonna shit when he finds the body missing!" whispered Brian as they clustered at the small table in the corner of the bar.

"And he won't want to tell anyone what's happened!" laughed Bob.

"I can't wait. I can't friggin' wait!" said Jim.

"It won't take long. He should notice it missing in a couple of days," noted Brian.

And so they waited. They waited and they waited. Two weeks passed without a hint from Pedley that anything was amiss. The anticipation was killing them. It got to the point where they were interrogating Jackson each time they met up with him. They kept asking him if anything was new or if everything was all right. He was actually starting to wonder why his friends were being so thoughtful and why they were so concerned about him. He thought that they must be really bored with the winter to be worried so much about his state of being.

Then one Saturday morning in late February it happened. Pedley woke up and found that his power was off. He checked his breaker box and found that the main switch had been thrown. He switched it back on and checked his refrigerator and personal freezer in the kitchen. Everything was still okay. That's when he thought of his other freezer and went out to the side room to ensure the two bodies inside were still frozen.

For about thirty minutes he was beside himself and in a real state of fear. He panicked and paced and hyperventilated. Then he sat down and had a good talk with himself. "Now think about it Jackson. Why would anyone take a body? Who would take a body?" And that's when he put the first pieces of the puzzle together. Nobody would take a body, except his asshole friends! "Now Jackson, play this right," he said to himself. "No more panic. You can do this. You can pull a 'Brian' on Brian!" He smiled as he grabbed a pencil and paper to work this thing out. He could do this, but he would need some help.

Actually it was quite simple to figure out who the key players were in the body-snatching caper. The four buddies who had been so concerned about his well-being in the past two weeks. "That's why they keep asking me if I'm okay. They're dying for me to find the body missing," Jackson chuckled to himself. "Damn I love those guys!"

Pedley decided that Father O'Reilly was not privy to this trick otherwise he would have been pumping him for information during the past month. He was also sure that Mary was not involved. She usually was more like a mother hen, chastising Brian for his practical jokes, but enjoying the results just the same. So he arranged a secret meeting with the priest and the teacher at his office for one o'clock.

When the two arrived, Pedley offered them each a coffee and then they sat down to talk. Initially, Father O'Reilly and Mary were horrified that Johnny Michael's body had been taken. Jackson, on the other hand, was more enthused about his plan to retrieve the corpse. It did not take long for the others to begin to enjoy the conspiracy, after all they were rescuing Johnny from God knows where, and at the same time doing something that would burst the bubble of joy that the four devils had been floating around in for the past month. By the end of the meeting they were all agreed. Not only would they find Johnny and take his body, but they would also not put it back in Pedley's freezer. The corpse would go into Father O'Reilly's freezer to rest safely until spring. The first step was up to Mary. She had to find out where they had hidden Johnny.

"That won't take long gentlemen. Brian hasn't mentioned a word of this to me, but I know how to handle him. He can function quite nicely on his diet of beer, but he has no fortitude when it comes to the real stuff. I'll go home and pour him a couple of stiff rye and gingers. I'll have all the details in a couple of hours," she said smugly and trotted off home.

When Mary arrived home it was very simple for her to cajole Brian into having a highball with her. She just turned on the charm and hinted coyly that there may be romance in the air. She laughed to herself because Brian would never learn that after a few rye and gingers he was not capable of any form of romance and only talked a good line before passing out. She didn't want to ask Brian directly about Johnny's body, so she skirted the issue with an elaborate story about Bob's wife, Sandra, and how she wanted to buy a massive ice cream cake for Victoria Day, but she needed a large freezer to store it in until May 24th. Without batting an eye, Brian told her that the RCMP and TranGas freezers were full of bodies and she should try Father O'Reilly. "Good idea!" Mary replied and they moved on to other topics. "Men," thought Mary, "It's a good job we don't care to participate in their little war games very often; otherwise it just wouldn't be fair. They are too easily conned by the average woman."

By the time Brian passed out on the chesterfield, Mary was sure she knew the location of the missing corpse. She called Jackson and they agreed to meet Father in an hour, after TranGas shut down and Jim had left for the day. Mary stopped by TranGas while Jim was still finishing up his paperwork for the week. She went on the pretence that Brian had forgotten his warmest mitts somewhere and asked if she could look in the adjoining building. While she was in the room she unlocked the back door so they would be able to enter after Jim left. Then she said good bye to Jim telling him that Brian must have forgotten his mitts somewhere else. He nodded and waved absentmindedly as he was concentrating on the pile of invoices on his desk.

Jim left his office a few minutes later. He locked the front door and glanced over his shoulder to ensure that the lights were off in both buildings then he drove straight to the hotel to unwind. Mary, Father O'Reilly and Jackson were in Mary's truck and waiting just down the road. As soon as Jim drove off they were veering around to the back of the TranGas property. They went in the back door with two flashlights and pulled on the lid of the freezer.

"Damn, it's locked!" said Pedley.

"We're outta luck," groaned Father.

"No wait, we're not dealing with geniuses here. Plus they really had no concern that someone was ever going to steal the body back. They just locked it so no one would open it and have a heart attack," reasoned Mary.

"So think, where would Jim keep his keys?" Father O'Reilly wasn't very good in this kind of situation and was starting to panic.

"In his desk!" both Mary and Jackson said in unison.

They found a pile of keys in the top drawer of Jim's desk and it only took a few minutes of trying various keys to unlock the freezer. Mary raced back into the front office and replaced the several rings holding all the keys.

They carried Johnny out to Mary's truck, drove over to the parish, and gently placed the body in Father's freezer. Father said a few words over the corpse and then shut the lid, locked the freezer and put the key in his jacket pocket, zippering it up and nodding knowingly at his companions. They wouldn't make the same mistake as the others. This key was secure.

Chapter Sixteen

March is a neurotic month, as it can be in many places around the world. It can continue on with the desolate weather of the previous two months, or it can be a wet and blizzardy four weeks, if an early spring is about to descend. Once in awhile it can surprise everyone and be beautiful. This year it was being kind to the residents of Everet. Every day was sunny and clear. The snow sparkled brightly and could literally blind anyone who was outside too long without sunglasses.

Mary was spending every weekend cross-country skiing with her students and friends. The weather was perfect and they had worked hard creating trails in the firebreak that surrounded town.

Every town and city in northern Canada, and many others throughout the continent, have constructed a firebreak around the community.

The concept is simple. When a forest fire travels close to a community, its path is obstructed by a wide constructed clearing that surrounds the town. It resembles a circular road and heavy fire fighting vehicles can use it in times of danger; but normally after it has been cleared of trees and large brush, then grass and flowers are allowed to flourish, and it resembles a donut shaped meadow around the residential area.

Northern Canada can have as many as one thousand wildfires burning in the late spring and summer. They can range from one to over one hundred thousand acres in size. It is not feasible to fight fires of this magnitude, and only the ones that threaten communities are addressed. If the fire can be fought with water from airplanes and crews on the ground, then it can be tempered enough for a firebreak to protect the community. When the winds are high, and the ground is dry, fires can cover thousands of acres and the flames reach such heights that they can lick or jump miles ahead of the actual fire. Yukoners live with this seasonal reality and as with Mary and her fellow skiers, they often find recreational uses for this important protector.

A large number of snowmobiles also used the firebreak in winter, but there were no conflicts between the skiers and skidooers. They had mutually agreed that it would be skidoos to the left and skiers to the right. Mary would have preferred not to be disturbed by the noisy machines, but the firebreak ran for miles, so during an afternoon ski the heavy silence was only broken once or twice by engines zooming by.

Brian was out on a nearby lake ice fishing with his friends. Everyone was there, Eddie, Jim, Bob, Father O'Reilly and Jackson. They had also invited Brad Kincaid to join them. They were all enjoying themselves, but at the same time there was an edge to the gathering. Each group had been anxiously awaiting the other group to realize that the body was missing. It was driving everyone, except Brad, crazy with anticipation. Each was tempted to say something about Johnny that would trigger either Pedley or Jim to go and look in their freezers, but quite honestly it had not occurred to Jim to check on Johnny's body and Jackson already had done so and dealt with the situation quite cleverly.

It was Brad Kincaid who innocently triggered the spark that led to panic and horror within Brian's group. They were all sitting on old stools and benches around the ice hole, sipping hot toddies and chatting about nothing important when Brad asked Jim if he minded if Brad used the freezer in the side building at TranGas to store some moose meat that his neighbour had given him. Silence fell on the entire group as everyone waited for Jim's response.

"Well, normally I wouldn't mind, but head office is really monitoring expenses and I wouldn't be able to justify hooking it up." Jim was quite proud of his quick thinking, when the bomb fell.

"But Jim, it's already hooked up and running, and when I looked inside yesterday, I found it completely empty. It seems a real waste to have a freezer operating with nothing in it," replied Brad.

It was probably one of the hardest moments in Father O'Reilly and Jackson's lives. They had to continue sitting there, stone faced and fishing. After all, this was mediocre conversation about a mediocre subject. They did not dare to look up at any of the faces in the circle for fear of exploding with mirth. Rather they each sat still, staring at the fishing hole, and jiggling their rods once in awhile.

The other four conspirators had to also try and remain nonchalant. The silence was deafening. Poor Brad was the only person wondering what on earth was going on and why did Jim not respond to his comment about the empty freezer. People did favours for each other all the time around here. This was the last time he was going to try and be sociable with this crowd.

"I'm sorry Jim. I certainly don't want to put you in a tight spot. It's just that the meat is important for my family," murmured Brad.

"No, no Brad. It's not a problem. Of course the meat is important. As a matter of fact, you go and pick it up now and I'll meet you at the office so you can put it in the freezer today," answered Jim.

"That's great Jim. I know my neighbour wants it out of his freezer as soon as possible," Brad said.

Eddie jumped in to make things seem normal. "Come on Brad, I'll go with you to help bring it over to TranGas," and he jumped up and almost carried Brad off to the truck.

"Geez," thought Brad, "these guys go from cold to hot in a split second. No matter how hard I try, I just don't understand people. I'll never learn to be sociable and act normal, 'cause this sure seems damn weird to me!"

"Brian, you come with me," said Jim, "We should check and make sure the freezer is running properly."

"Good idea Jim!" answered Brian as he tried to walk rather than frantically race to his truck.

Within three minutes Father O'Reilly and Jackson were the only two left fishing at the ice hole. They had to remain calm and innocent until all the trucks were out of sight, and then it began. They could not speak. They could hardly breathe. Father managed to say something about trying to focus on reciting the books of the Bible and Jackson said he was silently trying to list the Criminal Code statutes through it all. They were roaring with pleasure. Finally the rogues knew that the freezer was empty. Let the games begin!

Brian and Jim arrived at the propane office at the same time and rushed to the freezer.

"Let me get the key," said Jim.

"Why?" asked Brian, "It's obviously unlocked!"

They raced into the far room and opened the ice box. It was truly empty. Johnny Michael was gone. They dragged their feet back to the front office and sat at Jim's desk. It was Brian who had the strength to speak first.

"Where is he? Who would do this?" Brian pondered.

"The only person who would be the least bit interested in that body is Jackson Pedley. Think about it. Even if someone else saw it, they wouldn't take it! It had to be Pedley," analysed Jim.

"But Jackson is so easy to read. He didn't budge at the ice hole. I don't think he could have controlled himself if he had taken Johnny," said Brian.

"Well there's a quick way to find out," said Jim, "if Jackson took the body then there's only one place that he'd put it."

"Of course, back in the RCMP freezer!" smiled Brian.

They went outside and hopped into Jim's truck. When they arrived at the police station, they entered the outer building and opened the police freezer. They stood there staring in disbelief. There was only the one body that had been in the freezer before Johnny's demise. They went as far as to lift the remaining body up in case Jackson had hidden Johnny under the original corpse. They were now truly horrified. Johnny Michael was missing and it was their fault. What were they going to do?

Chapter Seventeen

*W*hile the original conspirators prayed vehemently for record low temperatures and eternal winter, Jackson, Mary and Father O'Reilly waited anxiously for the spring thaw and Johnny's looming funeral ceremony. Brian was a wreck and he tossed and turned every night through April. There were times when Mary actually felt sorry for him, especially if she turned in bed to find him up and wandering around the house in the middle of the night; but then she would remind herself that he had stolen a body and she would roll over smiling and go back to sleep.

None of the four could sleep or eat properly, which actually pleased Bob and Eddie's wives enormously, since both had been growing substantial beer bellies over the winter. Jim and Brian could not even discuss the matter anymore, it was too distressing. So there was this truce of silence, while each hoped that another would solve the mystery or better yet some miracle would occur and the body would suddenly reappear.

Unfortunately, or fortunately, depending on your perspective, the only thing that did happen was that both Bob and Eddie slimmed down to weights they had not seen for over a decade. Everyone kept telling them how good they each looked, but the overpowering stress of the missing body, allowed neither man to enjoy their new bodies or the multitude of compliments coming their way.

It was truly the longest six weeks of their lives. They had decided to keep their mouths shut until Pedley and Father O'Reilly began making arrangements for the funeral. They knew that arrangements would begin a week prior to the actual burial, and then they would have to face the music. The funeral was set for the first week in May. They waited. Johnny's family sent word that several members would attend and made reservations at the hotel. They waited. The hole was dug at the small graveyard and drainage channels chiselled to allow for runoff of any excess water. They waited. Mary ordered the flowers for the church. They waited. Father asked them to help choose a coffin from his catalogue. This almost killed them. It was excruciating for the entire group. They were sure that they were all going directly to hell.

The night before the funeral the four met at Eddie's garage. They could not bear the thought of facing Johnny Michael's family at the hotel.

The guilt was overwhelming. It was the first time for these kind and honest men to experience the enormous weight that the conscience can place on a person. Real guilt and shame are very overwhelming states with absolutely no cure except confession.

"Jesus Christ!" said Brian, "Why hasn't either of them checked the freezer yet?"

"What are they going to do in the morning, with everything ready to go and no corpse for the coffin?" groaned Jim.

"We're assholes. Anything for a laugh, eh? Well nobody's laughing now. We're dead meat!" Eddie was shaking his head and looking at the ground.

"The worst part isn't his actual body, it's the family. His whole goddamn family is here! We loved this guy and we've ruined his final moment with his family. Shit!" yelled Brian as he rose and started pacing the garage.

They each chose to deal with the impending doom in their own way. Bob actually went running for the first time in years and ran up the highway until he collapsed. It took him hours to walk back to town. Eddie polished and re-polished every tool and piece of chrome in the garage until the sun rose. Jim went home and for the first time in weeks, ate everything available in the kitchen. Brian rummaged through his storage boxes and found a copy of Dante's *Inferno* and read it cover to cover before sunrise. It was interesting that not one of them chose to have a drink of alcohol. It was as if they all wanted to be lucid for their executions.

Years later, not one of them could remember changing clothes for the funeral, nor could any one of them remember driving to the church, but to their credit all four men entered the church that morning to face the consequences of their actions. Mary was waiting for Brian by the back of the church.

"I know this is going to be tough. Let's get it over with Babe," she said as she took Brian's arm and led him down the aisle to the coffin surrounded with flowers.

There, laying placidly in satin and lace was Johnny Michael. He didn't look too bad considering his extensive travelling itinerary and the fact that he was still half frozen. There was no embalming in these isolated communities, so viewings were brief and burials quick.

"It's a miracle!" whispered Brian.

"What are you talking about now?" asked Mary, trying to hide her pleasure, "Pebbles and miracles, you are obtuse some times!"

The ceremony was short and typically formal. After all, the real ceremony had taken place months earlier on the porch of the hotel. Father said a few generic words about the deceased and mass was offered to the few practising Catholics in the pews. Brian noticed Jackson leaning forward from the pew behind them to whisper to Mary a couple of times, but he was in such a state of euphoric relief, that he just sat and floated through the entire ceremony in a sort of semi-conscious blissful calm.

Everyone followed the family to the grave-yard and Johnny was finally laid to rest. As everyone drove out of sight, Jim, Bob, Eddie and Brian stayed back. They had a job to do; one that most of us are denied in this era of shallowness and modern convenience. Silently, they each picked up a shovel and began to fill the grave. Tears streamed down the cheeks of each man. It was sad and it was tiring, but it was necessary and it was healing. Johnny was gone.

They did not think once about the past few weeks as they patted each other on the back and shook hands before leaving the graveyard. It had all been done in silence except for a few murmured good byes as they turned to their trucks.

Brian pulled in to the driveway at home. Mary had been waiting hours for him to return. She had carefully placed the 45 rpm that her sister had sent her for Christmas on the record player. It was a group called Hot Chocolate and her sister was sure she would love the single. She waited until she heard the truck door slam, counted to three, put the needle on the record and raced to the kitchen pretending to wipe the counter.

Brian entered the house and heard Mary singing along with the new song:

"I believe in miracles
Where you from
You sexy thing!

It took Brian a couple of choruses to catch on.

"Miracles! It's a miracle. It was you! Mary it was you!" he gasped.

Mary turned to him and said, "Are you angry?"

"Angry?" asked Brian. "You are a clever, brilliant, witty, fantastic woman! I'm not angry. I'm amazed, impressed, proud and more than a little jealous. Come here you sexy thing!" Then in typical Brian fashion and spirit he grabbed her and kissed her passionately.

"Nothing turns you on more than genius!" Mary whispered in his ear.

"You're damn right!" Brian answered. "Any face can be prettied up with some make up or a little surgery my dear. But our mind is a fantastic gift. As my grandfather used to say, 'you can't fix stupid'!"

IV

Where to Go from Here

Chapter Eighteen

By June, summer was well underway. The land had dried up from the spring runoff and the days were long and sunny. Mary was in good humour. There were only a few weeks of school left and then she would have two glorious months off. Brian was looking forward to her vacation as well. He received a lot more attention from Mary when she was on summer vacation. He was already looking forward to the wonderful lunches and dinners that he had experienced the previous summer. He had never really considered choosing a partner who would stay at home permanently, but the summer meals were his substitute for a two-month holiday.

Mary liked to cook when she had the time, and she was already making lists of ingredients and checking cookbooks for interesting recipes. She preferred the cookbooks with photos. It was difficult for her to imagine a dish simply from the written word.

Her sister was married and living in Bombay. This was quite extraordinary in 1976. There were not many Canadians living overseas. For Christmas, Mary had received a huge box from India loaded with spices and dried herb, most of which she had never seen before. Her sister had carefully labelled each container and included a beautiful cookbook. It was the most interesting present Mary had received that year and she was anxious to begin experimenting. Unfortunately, many of the recipes called for ingredients not readily available in Everet. Whitehorse had two huge grocery stores and a couple of ethnic shops as well. She was sure that she could gather everything required during a day of shopping. Most items were canned such as water chestnuts or coconut milk, so they would last for months.

It was Thursday night and she was marking the last of her senior students' exams when Brian came home. He had been out with Jim on an emergency service call and was a little shook up. There had been a gas leak in a kitchen stove and the owner of the house had not noticed. He was passed out at the kitchen table where a neighbour had found him. The neighbour had quickly pulled him outside and then called Pedley. Fortunately the man was going to be all right, but it had shaken Brian.

"I don't understand how it can happen. You know how propane stinks. He should have noticed the smell," said Brian.

"Maybe he did," answered Mary.

Brian raised his eyebrows, "Perhaps."

There were always a couple of tragedies each year with propane. A chemical odorant is added to the propane so a leak can be easily detected. It reminds most people of the smell of rotten eggs or a skunk's spray. For various reasons, some intentional and some accidental, people still die from propane poisoning. It is a peaceful way to die. People just fall asleep and the carbon monoxide kills them. This man was lucky, or not. No one would ever know for sure except him.

There was no leak to repair. One of the stove's top burners had been left on with no flame, so the gas was flowing into the kitchen. That did not mean it was intentional. Sometimes knobs are twisted when the stove is being cleaned or someone may bump into the stove and not notice that a knob as been turned. If it was not intentional, then the victim was lucky that he did not light a match. The whole house would have ignited instantly.

Brian and Jim had checked out the stove as a preventative measure and had opened all the windows in the house to give it a good airing. Pedley had taken the man to the cottage hospital. No one had been in the mood for a nightcap and Brian had come directly home.

"Listen, do you mind if I go up to Whitehorse this weekend?" asked Mary.

"Why not? I don't think we have any plans for the weekend," Brian replied.

"Sandra is driving up tomorrow night and I can tag along. She has to drop her car off for the warranty check. We'll drive back Sunday morning," explained Mary.

"Good. That means Bob and I can have some fun!" laughed Brian.

"You seem to be able to do that well enough when we're around," Mary smiled.

Brian chuckled as Mary turned on the stereo and started playing her favourite song.

I believe in Miracles, where you from, you sexy thing!

Brian laughed as he went to the bathroom to have a shower. Mary danced in the kitchen as she poured herself a rye and ginger. Then she went to pack a small bag for her weekend trip. She and Sandra always had a good time in the big city.

The girls arrived in Whitehorse about ten o'clock Friday night. The night had been clear so the road was dry and easy to navigate. There was more traffic on the roads in summer. Truckers could drive longer hours because of the additional hours of sunshine and with the summer gas stations and lodges open for the season, more assistance was available if they had engine problems.

The tourists were also beginning to make the pilgrimage to Alaska. It was clear that many of the visitors had been planning this once in a lifetime trip for a long time. Their campers and motor homes looked like tanks as they made their way up the Alaskan Highway.

The road was gravel and dirt, and local residents accepted the fact that their windshield would never be perfect. Within the first hundred miles of any Alaska Highway excursion, a stone would inevitably fly into your windshield and leave a smashed circular incision that would eventually create at least one crack that would travel across your entire window. In the south, a police officer often stops a car with a large crack in the windshield. Car insurance would not even consider covering broken windshields north of sixty and no one was expected to replace a window every time a stone flew into it. Most tourists had read extensively about the famous highway and the conditions, so many of the vacation vehicles arrived in Everet with the most inventive protection systems imaginable. Some had large screens bracketed across the entire front of a motor home. Others had covered the entire vehicle with cardboard. Many even had additional lighting systems on the front and the back of their homemade tank. They resembled alien spaceships landing as they approached. It was always fun to see what contraptions would arrive each summer. Sandra and Mary had enjoyed the drive, laughing at various inventions they passed along the way.

No trip in summer was uneventful; there were too many visitors around. Mary and Sandra had stopped to help one couple with a flat tire. They were an older, retired couple from Minnesota. A vast majority of the tourists were retired. It was an expensive and lengthy excursion which only those who had saved for a few years and had the time, could enjoy in style. Sandra and Mary had changed the tire for the couple. They had come well equipped but had forgotten that they might have to face situations that would challenge people half their age. It was fun. They all had a good chat. Mary and Sandra followed them for a few miles to monitor their safety and then passed by to speed on to Whitehorse.

They arrived too late for a nice supper at any of the good restaurants and agreed to dine out the following evening. They shared a room at a downtown hotel. After a few quiet drinks in the room they went to bed. They each had long lists of chores and shopping for the following day so they wanted to be up early.

The two women met back at the hotel the following evening. Mary was pleased with her shopping. She had found almost everything on her long list and was ready for a summer of Indian cooking. Sandra had bad news. Her truck required some extra work and would not be ready until Tuesday. It was not a problem for her, but Mary had to be back for school on Monday.

"I know you have to get back tomorrow Mary," Sandra told her, "So I called Bob and he's gonna find someone to bring you back."

"Thanks Sandra! Otherwise it would be kind of difficult to hitchhike with all this shopping." They went off for a nice dinner and bottle of wine.

The next morning Bob called their hotel room. He said he had solved the problem. A small Cessna airplane was flying down to Everet at noon and would take Mary and all her shopping along for the ride. This was a pleasant surprise. Mary and every other permanent resident north of sixty had many opportunities to fly in small Cessnas or single propeller planes, after all this was bush plane country. A lot of professional pilots would accumulate the required flight hours in the northern reaches of Canada before qualifying for positions as commercial pilots. Still, Mary was pleased. It was another beautiful day and the trip would take half the time by air.

The dealership had given Sandra a temporary loan truck, so they piled Mary's bags and boxes into the back of the truck and headed off to the Whitehorse airport. They drove to the small hangar area where the private planes parked and asked at the desk for the Cessna pilot who would be leaving shortly for Everet. The girl pointed to a short, stalky man who was cleaning the windows of his small aircraft.

"No!" said Mary, as she stopped in her tracks.

"What's the matter?" asked Sandra.

"That's Kevin Anderson!" replied Mary.

They both knew Kevin. He was the principal of Mary's school and a really nice guy; a good family man with a great sense of humour. He was also a good teacher and administrator, but a bit of an absent-minded professor type. He was the kind of person who is always asking if anyone had seen his keys or his wallet.

He had been taking flying lessons for a couple of years and finally passed the exam the previous weekend. The staff had bought him a funny pilot's hat to celebrate. It was brown leather with goggles and looked like something out of a 1940 war movie. He had loved it and had worn it to school all week. Now here he was in Whitehorse, wearing the silly hat and cleaning the windows of the old Cessna that he had bought last summer in anticipation of being licensed soon.

"What am I going to do? He's my boss! I have to fly with him! My God he must have only two solo hours under his belt!" groaned Mary.

"It'll be okay. You know these small planes, they fly so low that you can jump out with no parachute if something goes wrong," consoled Sandra.

"I know, but with our luck I'll be jumping out over Inuvik! The man has no sense of direction. It took him six months to navigate through the school building for God's sake," Mary was scanning the airport for other planes.

They walked over to greet Kevin. He was so excited and happy to be Mary's chauffeur for the trip that Mary felt badly for having doubts about his ability. They loaded up the back of the plane with all her items and then they hopped into the plane. Sandra stood waving good bye as they taxied off to the short, private runway. Mary looked back at Sandra and pretended to be chewing her nails in fear. Sandra laughed and held up her hands with all fingers crossed. And then suddenly, they were off.

It was a gorgeous day and the view over the city was marvellous. As she was looking out the window and trying to identify particular buildings, Kevin tapped her shoulder. She turned to look at him and he handed her a map.

"You can be the official navigator, Mary," he stated.

Although Kevin and Mary were professional colleagues, they had also become good friends. They quickly recognized the chemistry between them that leads to comfortable conversations, similar to members of the same family. They would often tease each other at work and play practical jokes on one another. Only last week, Mary had completely taped up his office telephone with masking tape and then went to find him in the gymnasium to say that the superintendent had called and would be calling back in five minutes. Kevin had rushed to his office, and Mary had rushed to the staffroom. As soon as she saw Kevin enter his office, she called him from the other room. She had laughed hysterically as she watched Kevin trying to rip the tape off his telephone. He had been in a complete panic thinking that his boss was calling and would not get an answer from the school. It made work fun. This flight was a different matter and Mary was not having any fun at the moment.

"What are you talking about?" hollered Mary over the noise of the engine, "I don't know how to navigate a plane!"

"Sure you do! We're just going to follow the highway most of the way. Now where is the highway?" he pondered.

Mary groaned and shook her head. When she realized that he really was looking for the highway, she started to search the ground carefully.

"There it is! That's the junction to right," she yelled.

"To the west," Kevin corrected.

"There!" Mary pointed with exasperation.

They followed the highway as Kevin had promised, except for the huge bends around high ground, when Kevin would fly straight over the small mountain and meet up with the road again on the other side. Mary was nervous every time this occurred, and would sigh with relief when she could see the highway again. Just as they had both agreed that they must be very close to Everet, they greeted a large, white cumulus cloud. As they entered the cloud, Mary's heart started to race. It was not a comfortable feeling to have no vision whatsoever. Rather than enjoy the privilege of such an experience, Mary broke out into a cold sweat. When they flew out of the cloud she sighed with relief. She could see the ground again, but not the highway.

"Where's the road?" she asked Kevin.

"I don't know. You're the navigator!" he answered with a smile.

"How could he be so flippant?" Mary thought, but she said, "Okay, we were flying on the left side of the road."

"On the east side," Kevin corrected.

Mary rolled her eyes and continued, "Are we flying south? Make sure we're heading due south."

"We are," said Kevin.

"Okay then, the road can only be on our left or right, excuse me east or west," she reasoned.

"Veer west Captain," she commanded.

They were lucky. In a few minutes Mary saw the road again and this time they flew low and followed it closely. Both had been left a little rattled when they emerged from the cloud. After flying for another half hour, Mary was concerned. They should have arrived in Everet by now. She thought that they must be following the highway south of Everet and suggested that they turn around. Kevin on the other hand thought they were still north of town. He believed that if they turned around they would end up back in Whitehorse.

"Well, what do we do then?" asked Mary.

"Simple," replied Kevin, "we check a mile post."

The Alaska Highway starts in Dawson Creek, British Columbia. The starting point is 'Mile 0'. Each mile is marked with a white post and a number. This continues right up to Fairbanks at mile post 1322. They knew the mile post at Everet, so as soon as they read the next post they would know if they were north or south of town. It was a practical suggestion, but not achieved easily from the air. Each time they saw a post, Mary would look back to read the number. The problem was that by the time they were at an angle for Mary to read the number it was too far away to see properly.

Suddenly without warning, Kevin slowed the plane and flew down directly above the highway.

"What are you doing?" yelled Mary.

"Is anything coming your way?" Kevin shouted back.

Without waiting for an answer, he slowed the plane to make a landing on the highway. Mary was covering her eyes and screaming. Kevin was saying something about 'not to worry' and 'this was done all the time'. It was a very good landing had it been on a regular runway, but this unorthodox choice had shocked and terrified Mary.

"You're out of your mind! This is NOT done all the time. I have never met up with a Cessna on the Alaska Highway!" she shouted.

Kevin was laughing.

"Why do all the men in this country laugh at everything?" yelled Mary.

As the plane rolled to a stop at the next mile post and the engine quieted, Kevin turned to her and said, "Because my dear, there are only two types of people on earth, women and children."

Each agreed with this statement. Mary saw it as a derogatory comment about men. Kevin saw it as an insult to women. Neither person realized that the other held a differing point of view, so there was no ensuing argument.

They got out of the plane to stretch their legs and check the post.

"You're right. We're south of Everet," admitted Kevin.

As he spoke, they both looked south and saw the distinctive cloud of dust that followed every vehicle travelling the highway. It reminded Mary of old western movies when the bandits could see the posse chasing them from miles away.

The plane with its wingspan was as wide as the road. Only low vehicles would be able to pass by under a wing. If they didn't do something quickly they would create a very difficult situation. There were often situations that halted traffic on the highway, like an accident or a washed out section, but it took a long time to be cleared or repaired. They each looked at each other, slightly panicked, as they realized that there was no place to move the plane and a vehicle was fast approaching.

"Get in!" yelled Kevin, "Quick!"

They both jumped into the Cessna and slammed the doors. Kevin started to taxi.

"You are totally insane!" shouted Mary.

"They're at least a half mile away," retorted Kevin.

As they picked up speed, Mary's heart was racing. The section of the road was straight for another three or four hundred yards and then there was a sharp curve to the right. She kept her focus on the dust cloud now approaching very quickly. Kevin was pushing the plane to its limit, but that limit was limited! It was an old and small engine. They were still on the ground when the red jeep rounded the corner and headed toward them. Kevin was leaning back and pulling the throttle with him. Then it happened. They lifted off and flew so close to the roof of the jeep, that Mary could see the terrified eyes of the driver only a few feet in front of her. She looked back to see if the vehicle was okay. They were slowing down but the jeep was still on the road. "Thank God for small miracles," she thought.

Kevin turned the plane north and they flew back to Everet in silence. When they landed at the airport and jumped from the plane, Mary was still shaking. Brian was waiting for her. He started to ask them how the flight had been, but Mary just glared at Kevin and then back at Brian and said, "Don't ask!"

Brian loaded her shopping into his truck and they drove back to town.

"What happened Mary?" he asked, "You're in a foul mood."

"You won't believe it when I tell you. Just give me a few minutes to unwind."

"Wanna stop at the hotel?" Brian offered.

"Absolutely! I need a drink!" and that was all she said until they reached the bar and their usual corner table.

Chapter Nineteen

They were just ordering their first drink when Eddie came and joined their table.

"I just heard the damndest story from two guys filling up at the station," he said, "Apparently they were rounding the bend near the junction, and coming straight at them was a Cessna! Right on the highway!"

"What was it doing on the road?" asked Brian.

"They don't know. It taxied straight at them and then lifted off just seconds before hitting their jeep. Scared the shit out of them!"

"I guess so! You ever heard of such a thing Mary?" Brian asked, with a twinkle in his eye.

Mary dropped her head to the table and groaned loudly.

"They're coming over to join us after they finish at the station," Eddie continued, "I can't wait to hear all the details."

So what should have been a quiet Sunday afternoon in preparation for the coming week of work, turned into a social event. The two men in the jeep arrived, followed by Jim, Father O'Reilly and Pedley. Bob, who was always at the hotel, join them. After hearing the story several times and roaring every time at each detail, Brian called Kevin and convinced him to come down to the hotel to defend himself.

Once Mary had downed a few ryes and Kevin had joined them, even she could begin to see the humour in the scene. As time went on, it was to become one of the more memorable events in her life and she would think fondly of Kevin every time the memory unwrapped itself and floated gently to the surface of her mind. She would think of it often during the summer of '76. Each time she opened a can of Asian vegetables or a packet of powdered coconut milk, she would envision them strewn across a lonely stretch of the Alaskan Highway, never to be added to a recipe. "Shakespeare was wrong," she would think. "Life is not a stage. It's more like a circus tightrope act. Yes, life is a tightrope and we have to work hard to keep our balance," she would think to herself as she stirred a new foreign delight.

The difficulty with Mary's particular circus act was that she was followed by an extreme athlete who was constantly bouncing on the rope and taking unnecessary risks, which tended to affect her balance. She often wished that Brian would slow down, on the other hand, if he did calm down, she would probably find him mundane. "God certainly does have a sense of humour," she would think to herself. "I hope that he's enjoying the show!"

When she would explain her analogies to Brian he would always understand her thinking. He liked analyzing life.

"Of course He's enjoying it Mary! Think of it this way. Anyone who creates something wants to see it operating the way they imagined it would. Well if God gave us this great sense of humour, then we have to put it to good use for the audience. I'm sure all those angels up there are pretty experienced critics! I like to think that we have a prime time slot," and he chuckled and chortled over his own comments as she shook her head and studied him. His wit always warmed her heart. His antics didn't.

One summer evening, they were eating a particularly hot curry that Mary had made. Brian was perspiring, his face was red and tears were rolling down each cheek. He had asked Mary for a box of tissues, as he was forced to blow his nose after every few mouthfuls.

"If it's too hot, don't eat it," Mary said.

"It's evil," replied Brian, "It's killing me and I can't stop eating it. Is it some magical concoction? Are you trying to kill me? "

Mary smiled and got up to get more water. Brian gulped a full glass and then dug into the curry again.

"When is the summer over?" he asked, "I need to get back to a healthy diet of hamburgers at the hotel!"

Much to their chagrin, the summer did pass all too swiftly. It was the last week of August and school would begin again, after the first weekend in September. Mary had already been over to the school to prepare her classroom and meet the new teachers.

There was a core of permanent residents in Everet, and then there was an 'outer' core; people who would come up and live there for a couple of years, and then move south again. Each June the school staff would say good bye to a few colleagues and each August they would greet their replacements. Nothing was totally permanent in the Arctic. The conditions were simply too severe for most people to consider putting down deep, permanent roots.

Mary had not thought about it much, but she supposed that she too would move on at some point in time. The winters were too long and too cold to consider retiring in Everet. The north was a form of addiction. Perhaps residents did not take one day at a time, but certainly they considered one year at a time. With each passing year spent in the Arctic, came a sense of achievement and a development of personal strength. People would proudly say to themselves, "not many of those wimps down south could endure this country!"

Chapter Twenty

*A*utumn was Brian's favourite season. It was a short season in the north, and that made it more important to enjoy every moment of it. The tourists were gone and locals had the country to themselves again. The mosquitoes and black flies were also gone. Brian would often comment that he could not decide which was more annoying the flies or the visitors. Mary had a terrible reaction to mosquito bites and would tell him that there was no decision to be made. Mosquitoes were evil and she hated them.

Since Mary could not cope with the summer bugs, autumn was also the best time for the couple to go camping. They spent almost every weekend out of town in different locations, usually near a river or stream. One of the joys of the Yukon and its isolation, were the camping trips. There were no public camping grounds, no fees to pay, no public showers or communal cook areas; just the beauty and peacefulness of the private spot where you chose to stop.

Brian and Mary usually went camping alone. Brian was such a social creature, that they had agreed to use the autumn excursions as 'couple' time. They both truly enjoyed these weekends. They would bring more than enough food for the two days, but usually they caught enough fish for both evening meals. Fresh rainbow trout, fried in butter, over an open fire and eaten after a day of mountain air and activity is not merely a pleasure but a privilege. Mary and Brian would often count their blessings during these autumn weekends. It was a nice time of year for both of them.

Brian and his friends had enjoyed a relatively quiet summer. There had certainly been barbecues and parties, but the 'freezer' incident had really traumatized each one of them, so there had been no planning of any type of practical joke.

It had actually been a summer of many serious discussions. Folklore speaks of a seven-year itch and of predictable times of change in a person's life. The summer of '76 must have seen some planets align, because several friends were contemplating change. It needed to be discussed.

Jackson was the first to ask his friends for advice. After the Japanese group had departed, and Ottawa had shown its pleasure with Constable Pedley and his excellent planning of the short tour of Everet, there had followed a couple of offers. They were exciting prospects, but they also involved some serious thought and consideration.

Early in July, a representative from Bombardier, the large snowmobile manufacturer, had flown up to Everet to meet with Jackson. He had asked Pedley to consider a career with the corporation. Jackson would be based out of Montreal.

Then in August, two men from the British Columbia and Yukon Lumbermen's Association had also come to town and met with the local hero. They had offered him a similar position. This job was based in Vancouver.

As Socrates had noted more than two thousand years earlier, the world of private enterprise is more efficient than government. It took the bureaucracy of the RCMP and Ottawa much longer to respond to the success of the Japanese visit. This is normal. Bombardier and the lumber companies had all received lucrative contracts, while the bureaucracy had only received gratitude. Money truly does speak louder than words.

In late September Jackson had received word from his immediate boss that he would be transferred the following June to a small coastal town in the northwest of British Columbia, and to a corporal's position. From a huge bureaucracy this was major recognition for a young man only five years in the force. Compared to the offers from Bombardier and the Lumber Association it seemed trite.

So began the season of Pedley's Dilemma. At first, Brian, Bob, Jim and Eddie had enjoyed the conversations. The pros and cons of each offer were weighed and discussed at length. The security of a government job versus the tenuous positions out in the real world; the excitement of world travel versus the dreary rain of the west coast, and most vehemently discussed were the high salary offers from the business world versus the standard, middle class salary of the RCMP. It had all led to many evenings of vibrant and interesting discussion. By October it was no longer interesting. Each time the group gathered for a drink, it felt like a re-run of last season's show. It had become boring. They wanted Jackson to stop waffling and make a decision.

Brian was astute when it came to reading people. He told Mary that he wished the discussions would end because Pedley had already made his decision.

"What has he decided?" she asked.

"He doesn't know that he's decided yet," said Brian, "but he's going to stay with The Force."

"How do you know that?" continued Mary.

"Because anyone truly made for the business world would have jumped at the Bombardier offer," Brian explained, "He'd already be out of here. Five years on the salary they offered him would equal a typical pension fund in full. Some people are mathematically challenged, and just don't have the personality type to take a risk. No, Pedley will be a Mountie until the day he retires."

"There's nothing wrong with that," commented Mary.

"Not at all," said Brian, "I just wish that he'd hurry up and make the conscious decision so we could stop talking about it all the time!"

"The northwest coast sucks though," said Mary.

"That's the way bureaucracy works my dear. It gives you one cup of honey plus one cup of vinegar. Here's a promotion! Now go to hell!"

Mary smiled at Brian's cutting remark, and then they both settled down to read their winter books.

Each of them had been sent a large box of books from their mothers. The anticipation of so much good reading helped to alleviate the thoughts of the coming winter.

Mary had chosen *The Exorcist* as her first winter read. There were no bookshops in the north. People had to rely on family or friends to supply current reading material. Mary's mom had told her that everybody down south had been talking about the book for a couple of years, so Mary decided she had better bring herself up to date.

Brian on the other hand, had decided to revisit plays. He had asked his mother for a variety of Russian and English playwrights. He had decided on *The Importance of Being Ernest* to begin the new season. He loved Oscar Wilde. "Only the shallow know themselves."

Late November found both Mary and Brian curled up and reading while the north winds blew and winter settled in. It also found Brian laughing in his sleep at Oscar Wilde's wit and Mary sleeping with the lights on and jumping at every small creak or groan the house made during the night. She was not enjoying *The Exorcist*.

The last Friday of November everyone met after work at the hotel for dinner and drinks. Jackson announced that he was staying with The Force and transferring next year. Brian winked at Mary and she covered a smile with her napkin. Everyone congratulated their friend and talk shifted to the northwest coast. Almost everyone had a story of a visit to the area or a relative who had lived there.

Then the conversation switched to the upcoming Everet bonspiel. It was the biggest event of the year for the curling club. Teams came from all over the north. The roster had to be drawn up. The ice prepared. The bar at the club stocked for extensive socializing. Trophies polished and prizes purchased. Accommodation had to be arranged. The hotel was only had twenty rooms. More than twenty teams from out of town were already registered. That meant eighty people needed to be housed and fed for the three-day tournament.

Mary had her eye on the B Event trophy and prizes. She came from a long line of B Event champions. As far as she was concerned it was the only event to win in any bonspiel. B Event champions were special teams.

A curling bonspiel begins with all teams equal. Teams play their first game. Winners of the first game stay in the A event. Losers move to the B Event. Losers of the B event move down to the C Event, and so on. Each team is guaranteed three to five games, depending on the number of events. At any given time, A Event teams have not lost a game. B Event teams have only lost one game. This pattern continues down to the last event. Games are played round the clock. Parties continue round the clock also. The bar never closes during a bonspiel.

The A Event teams tend to be serious. They'll have the obligatory drink after each game and then go back to their rooms to rest and discuss strategy. Mary's Scottish heritage and upbringing had always made her chuckle at these teams. Her grandfathers had told her many a time, that a bonspiel was a measure of much more than curling skills. It was a measure of strength of a character and constitution. A true bonspieler should be able to socialize with the best and still win a top event. In essence this meant curling and partying around the clock for seventy-two hours and winning the B Event. Once in a blue moon such a hardy team would manage to win the A Event. It was a glorious moment to stagger up to accept the A Event trophy, the room booming with cheers and hoots from teams befriended during the bonspiel, take the coveted trophy in hand and smile at all the serious teams who had tried so hard and had so little fun.

Curling teams pay hefty fees to enter a bonspiel and the hosting club adds a substantial amount of money from their own purse. Annual bonspiels are a matter of pride and tradition. The prizes have to be good. For the past two weeks, this year's prizes had been on display at the curling club and Mary had fallen in love with the B Event first prize. It was four paintings by a well-known northern artist who Mary really liked. If they could win the B event then she and Brian would have two of his works.

She wanted those paintings. She also knew that she would have to try and forget about them. Curling is like gambling. If someone plays poker when they're broke, and they have to win, the odds are against them. The only time the win is big is when the winner already has lots of money. "God and his sense of humour again," Mary would think. So she had to make herself forget about the paintings and just have fun and concentrate on the games for the sake of the game. She also had to hope that Brian would not waste all his shots. That man could read people but he sure couldn't read ice! She smiled as she looked across the table at Brian.

Brian was wearing Pedley's RCMP hat and Jackson was wearing Brian's TranGas cap. Bob was singing, 'There'll always be an England' and Father O'Reilly was covering both his ears. Jim was talking seriously to Eddie who was listening intently, but had a straw sticking out of each ear. Mary looked over at Sandra. Sandra looked back at her and said, "God I love them!" Mary rolled her eyes and nodded with a grin.

It was early evening when Brian and Mary arrived home. Mary started pouring a hot bath.

Brian picked up the book he had started yesterday. It was a play by Chekhov. As Mary stepped into the tub she could hear Brian yell to her, "These damn Russians! The stories are good, but each character has about a hundred different names. I need to start a flow chart to keep track of who is who!"

"Maybe that's the point!" Mary hollered back, "Maybe you need to find the essence of the characters and forget about the names."

"Bull shit doesn't always baffle brains, my dear!" he yelled back.

She laughed as she lay back to relax.

Chapter Twenty-One

*T*he curling bonspiel weekend arrived and the town of Everet was bustling with activity. When the adult population of a community increases by fifty percent overnight, the service industry is stretched to the limits. Eddie and Jim had taken on extra staff. Bob and Sandra had been busy for weeks, fine tuning menus and helping the restaurant staff to prepare as much as possible in advance. Three officers from Whitehorse had come down to help Pedley for the three day stint, and more importantly, to enter the event as the RCMP team.

The Everet Community Council had decorated the street lights with sparkly curling rocks and brooms. At each end of town they had hung huge banners welcoming the weekend guests to the Everet Annual Bonspiel. The Ministry of Transport snowploughs had made a meticulous run of town ensuring that all the roads were clear and accessible.

The curling club had contracted the hotel to run their bar and supply small meals and snacks at the club. They had made this arrangement a few years back. Although the bar was a good money maker, the food was a huge undertaking. Everet was so small that it was the same people who were on the curling club executive, the community council and who were the owners of every small business, so they had agreed to contract the food and drink out to the hotel and Bob gave a percentage of the profits back to the curling club.

Mary and Brian had prepared their outfits the weekend before the bonspiel. To serious curlers, the outfit is extremely important. There are numerous superstitions entwined with curling and each individual curler as well as every cohesive team had their own code to consider. There are special sweaters, a variety of club pins, special pants and knee pads, leather McIntosh boots, gloves, sliders, brooms and in particular for Mary's team, there were lucky socks.

Mary had been raised in a curling culture and she carried on with the rules of her ancestors without question. So for the Richardson team members, the socks worn for the first game had to be worn continuously for the entire bonspiel. Under no circumstance could any member of the team change their socks or worse yet, remove their socks.

Initially Brian had difficulty with the 'removal of socks' rule. He had been quite entertaining with his complaints during their first year together. Everyone had enjoyed his moaning to Mary about needing fresh socks and how difficult it was to shower with his socks on his feet. Mary had laughed with the crowds but would not budge on the rule. Then, near the end of that first year, they were in the last bonspiel of the year. It was very early on a Sunday and they were scheduled for a game at four o'clock in the morning. Bonspiel rosters continue round the clock at small clubs. Brian had gone home to shave and freshen up before the game. Without thinking, he had put on clean socks and raced back to the club. It was probably the worse game he had ever played. He wasted every one of his shots and although Mary had tried to take up the slack, they had lost the game and the B event.

Curling is a notoriously polite game and curlers generally display fine sportsmanship. They are humble in their victories and magnanimous in their defeats. Mary's team had enjoyed the drinks purchased by the victors and everyone from both teams had consoled Brian on his poor performance in the game. Every time Mary had looked at him that morning, he was sure she knew that he had broken the team rule. Brian never did tell Mary that he had changed his socks, but it did not matter, because he vowed to himself never to change socks during a competition again. As with any superstition that is taken seriously, people need to accumulate stories and experiences to justify their behaviour. Brian had his personal reasons now for never changing socks during a bonspiel.

Their first game in the 1976 Everet Curling Club Bonspiel was at four o'clock on Friday afternoon. It was a nice time to draw your first game. Everyone had arrived from out of town. Several teams had already played their first games so the ice had been read by some and advice could be given. The curling club was busy and full of warmth and conversation. Old friends were connecting. Many people had not seen each other since the last bonspiel of the season eight months ago.

Brian was in his glory. He was also busy in his role as president of the curling club. Although jobs had been delegated and most of the work had been done in advance, it was still important to oversee the event. It was also important to greet each team and act as primary host.

While Brian mingled with everyone and welcomed guests, Mary sat down with Father O'Reilly to chat and discuss the condition of the ice before the first game. The fourth member of their team was a new teacher at the school. Her husband worked on offshore oil rigs. He was on a six-week haul and so Mary had invited Lillian to join the team. Lillian was from Scotland and her thick Scottish brogue added nicely to the atmosphere.

Lillian enjoyed a good party, so Mary was expecting Brian and Lillian to be in rare form for the three-day event. It was nice to have Father O'Reilly as her third or vice skip. He was a solid curler, a fun team member and more importantly, not quite as excessive as Brian. She could count on him to be in better shape for each game than the other two team members. She still had her eye on the B event prize, which meant finding that magic balance between partying and playing a good game.

The first game went well. The teams were equally matched so the game was challenging. The entire game came down to Mary's last shot. Everyone in the clubhouse was watching as Mary and Father O'Reilly quietly discussed strategy before she threw the rock. Brian and Lillian were further up the ice, waiting to follow the stone to the other end. The opposing team was sitting with one stone on the outer circle and a few of their rocks acting as guards in front. Mary had to bring one of her stones in closer to the centre circle.

"I'd like to slide in past the front two rocks and just touch the blue," Mary was saying to Father.

"It's either that or tap our front guard stone in, which might be easier," replied Father.

"Easier and safer, but rather dull wouldn't you say?" smiled Mary rather slyly.

"Well if you're going to walk on thin ice, you might as well dance!" laughed Father, "Go for it Mary!"

Mary crouched to study the far end of the ice one last time, then positioned herself and smoothly delivered her last stone. She remained on her knees and followed the stone with her eyes yelling to Brian and Lillian to sweep, then stop, then sweep again. As it neared the far end of the ice, people began to stand and holler at each other in the clubhouse. All eyes were on the last stone thrown on ice number four. The stone slid past the first guard with less than an inch to spare, it curled and passed the second rock and slowly glided into place with Mary screaming to sweep and Brian and Lillian pounding the ice. Then Mary's stone stopped, sitting just a few inches from the centre point. The clubhouse was roaring with cheers. It was a fine moment. It defined the game and the reason these people were gathered.

Father put his arm around Mary and said, "An Englishman could never have made that shot!"

"Nor an Irishman!" piped in Lillian.

They went to shake hands with the losing team and to help put the rocks back in position for the next game.

"I don't mind losing to a shot like that one!" the opposing skip told Mary as they left the ice together and entered the clubhouse. Mary ordered a round for both teams and they sat down to relax and chat.

They played again at midnight, then at six on Saturday morning. After that there was another game at noon, then at eight on Saturday night. By midnight on Saturday they were exhausted. Mary had almost lost her voice. Everyone's shoulders were aching from the sweeping. No one had slept for more than two or three hours at a time. Brian really wanted to change his socks, but was afraid to mention it. They had won every game but one, so changing socks was out of the question.

Pedley's team had done well also and held the same record as the Richardson team. They were scheduled to play each other at four in the morning.

Father had been busy between games, with the Saturday evening mass and preparations for Sunday morning mass. Saturday evening mass had been crowded, since most of the congregation wanted to be present at the curling club on Sunday morning. If they lost to Pedley they would be out of the bonspiel. If they won the game, they would play in the finals at noon. Father was pleased that the schedule fitted with his work so well.

They were half way through the semi-final game with the RCMP team when it happened. Jim came racing into the club, hollering "Fire!" Within seconds men were calling to each other, throwing on parkas and running to their vehicles. All the men on the ice dropped their brooms and followed. An ominous silence descended on the group remaining in the club.

Unlike many people in the south, where idle curiosity can envelope fires and accidents, people north of sixty do not race to watch such scenes. They know from experience, that the victims will be friends and neighbours. There is no pleasure in standing on the sidelines and watching events unfold. It was best to stay out of the way and wait for the news.

It was sobering and no one wanted a drink. Water was boiled, tea and coffee served and people sat down to wait for information. There was quiet chatter about previous disasters. Comments about night fires and how much more dangerous they were, because no one would be awake to call it in as quickly as a daytime blaze. Mary just kept praying that it was one of their empty homes.

Outside the club, Jim was calling instructions to the men racing by. The firemen were given the location of the fire, the municipal drivers were told to bring the water trucks and Eddie and his crew were asked to drive the tow truck out to the fire in case a winch was needed. Everyone else sat in their trucks waiting to follow Jim to the blaze.

In times of crisis, there are those who panic and freeze, there are those who keep their head and react rationally to help and then there are others, sometimes heroes, sometimes fools, who leap with their heart. Brian leapt. As they pulled up to the small, log cabin, the adrenaline surged through his veins. He was consumed by one image, the two little girls trapped inside. While others struggled with equipment, Brian raced toward the cabin. One of the water trucks was already pumping and he ran into the spray to drench his body. Without a moment's hesitation

Brian entered the inferno. Bob and Pedley saw him at the same time and ran to stop him, but he had reacted so quickly that neither man reached the cabin door in time.

"The goddamn idiot!" Bob kicked hard at a log by his foot. "The cabin's been burning for more than an hour. No one's alive in there!"

A lifetime passed as Bob and Pedley paced and circled in front of the blaze. The flames were subsiding quickly with the water from four trucks now pounding the remnants of the small home. Jackson saw the movement at the door first. He took a step toward the cabin and then stopped. "Lord have mercy," he mumbled as Brian emerged.

Brian seemed confused for a moment. Then he saw Pedley, and with almost a sigh of relief, he walked toward his friend. In his arms hung the small, black bundle; barely recognizable, but for its size and one swollen, pink arm that the fire hadn't desecrated, hanging from the charred remains.

Brian stood in front of Pedley for a moment. He was clearly dazed. Then he raised his arms slowly and offered the child to Jackson, who accepted reverently. "Thank you Brian."

No one will ever quite remember the details of that moment. The death of a child is calamitous, the graphic reality is unbearable. Some men turned to vomit. Others dropped to their knees and sobbed. Others hid their head in their arms, against trucks or trees and heaved.

Brian and Jackson were staring into each other's eyes. Neither could bear to look at the child in Pedley's arms.

It was the doctor and nurse who finally joined the two men. Brian was wrapped in a blanket and the little girl's body was taken to the hospital van. Then the doctor and nurse walked Brian over to the ambulance. They laid him down and checked his vitals. Then the doctor prepared a sedative. The scene that followed would not surprise someone who has been in a war and standing on the killing fields after a battle. Young men wounded or traumatized by the horror of battle utter only one word as they lay dying or stunned. As Brian drifted off into sleep he whispered the same word, "Mommy . . ."

The hours dragged. Finally Father O'Reilly returned, filthy and exhausted. He was walking too slowly and slouching too severely for it to be good news. Everyone sat up as he came in and waited for him to speak. Mary slid a cup of coffee in front of him. He stared down at it for a long time before looking up at the anxious group around him.

"It's bad." he said.

"It was Brad Kincaid's cabin," he continued and stared back down at his coffee.

"Are they all right?" Mary asked.

Father looked up with tears running down his cheeks and shook his head.

"The girls?" someone asked.

He shook his head again. Shock and silence enveloped the room. No one asked Father any further questions. The room was in mourning and no further details mattered at the moment.

Mary was thinking of Brian and the other men out at the scene. It was one thing to hear news like this, it was quite another to work like mad to try and save your friends or to carry a tiny girl's body from a fire. She was thinking of the last time Brian had been in the cabin, happily placing gifts around the place last Christmas Eve.

"What kind of God takes children this way Father?" Mary murmured.

"The same God that gives them to us, my love," he answered.

Chapter Twenty-Two

*T*here are no professional therapy groups or trauma teams in the north to help survivors recuperate from disasters; only time and friends to help talk it through. Time was the first requirement. Not many of the witnesses wanted to talk much during the week that followed. Mary stayed close to Brian in case he needed her, but did not push him to speak. There were no words. Mary understood this. An entire young family erased within an hour. These were ordinary men trying to fight a fire and save a family; ordinary men finding the two young girls and having to deal with the reality of four deaths; ordinary men having to place four bodies somewhere and help deliver them someplace. She had to be around, without being around, while Brian worked through the torment.

While Brian processed events, Mary took over the duties of the curling club. The bonspiel had ended abruptly at three in the morning. No one had wanted to continue. Everyone told Mary to deal with prizes the way she saw fit. She and Sandra put the names of finalists for each event in a pot and drew names. They mailed or delivered the prizes to the teams chosen. No one really cared much, but it seemed right to bring the event to some kind of close.

Everyone thanked God that Jackson had brought three members of the force in for the weekend. It had helped everyone enormously to have four officers around during the disaster. The bodies had been sent immediately to Whitehorse via the RCMP twin otter. The officers had remained for a few more days to help with the cleanup of the cabin area and the paperwork entailed. No one was more thankful than Jackson for this additional help. Like everyone else in town, he was emotionally involved in this incident and it was hard for him to think logically. His colleagues took over for him.

Father O'Reilly was busy counselling everyone. He had been working alongside the men, so it was natural that many of them were able to speak with him first.

"She was so tiny, Father!"

"I know," he would answer.

"I had to carry her to the truck, Father. Jesus Christ!"

"I know."

He would cry with each of them before week's end.

The same week, Everet men spent an inordinate amount of time at the garage that housed the fire truck and water truck. They washed both trucks then spent several evenings wiping and polishing every nook and cranny. It seemed as though the fire had to be erased from both vehicles before it could begin to weigh lighter on their minds. They also needed to be with other witnesses. Traumatic events can never truly be captured with words, and it was somehow soothing to be with others who had experienced the flames, the bodies and the pain. Mary believed that it also helped to reassure each man that there was nothing else any of them could have done.

Ironically, the water truck had been at the cabins at two in the morning to fill the water tank that serviced the small group of cabins. Thirty minutes later Jim had waved and honked to the tank truck as they passed each other in town. They had stopped and hopped out of the trucks to chat. They were joking about the bonspiel and how everyone's schedule was upside down because of the odd hours. It was a clear night with a full moon. Jim saw the smoke rising from the cabin area as he spoke with the driver of the water truck. As a result, response time to the fire had actually been faster because of the curling event. Everyone was up, dressed and in one place when Jim had raced into the club calling for help.

These details were important to the community. It helped to alleviate the frustration and helplessness felt by everyone. No one could be blamed for not responding quickly or sleeping through the fire. There were actually more experts at the fire than usual since many of the visitors were volunteer fire department members in their own towns. These facts had to be pointed out numerous times during the healing process in the weeks that followed.

Brian had not shared his pain verbally with Mary, but he had not shut her out either. He had told her that there was nothing to say yet and had been quieter than usual, but he had also snuggled closer to her at night and held her hand more often when they sat together.

Christmas arrived a mere three weeks later. Life moved on. That is what people do through difficult times, they carry on.

For those who are not working with death on a daily basis, it is what strikes lay people as most amazing when a death is witnessed; how life just continues. The world does not skip a beat, let alone stop to mourn an individual death. Cars continue to drive past a fatal car accident, people continue to work in a hospital, and customers continue to shop near the scene of a recent heart attack. The person, who has seen their first death, wants to scream at the world to stop for one minute and to acknowledge the lost life for one second. The world does not operate at a miniscule level. It cannot celebrate every birth or lament over every death. Only those within each circle of family and friends are affected by the ripples of pain or joy that life regularly delivers.

Christmas was going to be tough. Mary was actually glad that it arrived so soon after the fire. It was going to be difficult no matter when it occurred, and she was a great believer in facing the music and getting through the pain as quickly as possible.

It was Christmas Eve and Brian and Mary were going to the hotel for a quiet evening with friends. Before leaving, they had decided to open one present each. Mary chose one of Brian's gifts and was thrilled to find two tickets to Hawaii for the spring break. They had never taken a winter holiday together. Brian said that it was great to give a gift that was also for him. Mary laughed and said he could give this kind of gift as often as he wished.

Brian chose a heavy box from Mary. She sat quietly while he opened it.

"What the hell is it?" he asked as he lifted it with both of his hands, "a part for my snow mobile or something? It weighs a ton!"

He unwrapped the box and lifted the top. Inside were about thirty pebbles of varying size and colour. The beautiful, smooth rounded ones found in old creek beds and mountain streams. Brian looked up at Mary with a warm smile.

"When did you gather these?" he asked.

"During our camping trips," she answered. "You're always talking about special pebbles so I thought I would collect a few nice ones just for you."

He held one up and studied it. They he ran his fingers through all of them.

"I love them!" he said as he looked up, "I love you!"

Mary was pleased that he liked the gift. She stood up and said, "Now perhaps you can explain the special pebble theory to me once and for all!"

"You got it!" he announced, "Come to the sink."

He filled the kitchen sink to the brim with cold water.

"Now come and observe," he said formally.

Mary stood beside him to watch the demonstration. He chose the largest stone from the box. It was really quite big. Mary had considered this one for some time before including it with the others. It was questionable whether it could be termed a pebble at all, but she had liked the markings on it.

"Now this one is beautiful, isn't it?" Brian lectured, "One would think that this would be a very special pebble. The shape is lovely, the colours superb and it is certainly the biggest pebble in the pond."

Mary nodded, as he continued, "Now, think of the water as life and the pebbles as individuals." He held the rock about a foot above the sink and dropped it. It hit the water with a heavy splash and water spilled over onto the counter and the floor. Mary jumped back and wiped her clothes. She was about to say something when Brian held up his hand and continued, "Bear with me, my dear. Now that huge rock had an affect on the water, but it was short lived and not very pretty, was it? You could say that it represents most famous people. They affect our lives on some superficial level. We know who they are. Many people talk about them when they die. Their funerals are packed with obligatory guests, and the mindless mob mourns them, but the size of the true void left by their departure is not measured by the big splashes they made.

Mary was more than a little lost at this moment, but she patiently waited while Brian continued.

"Now take this pebble," and he chose a smaller one, smooth and flat like a pancake. "This one can skip along the water beautifully. It will skim the surface and jump several times before finally sinking to the bottom of the pond," he let it fall quietly to the bottom of the sink. "This one is like most people. They race through life jumping through all the hoops and following all the rules and making numerous acquaintances along the way, but never really form many deep and lasting friendships or stop to appreciate the important things in life."

Mary now had an idea where this was heading and she leaned closer to Brian as he chose the final pebble. It took him some time before he lifted one from the box.

"Now I believe we have here a special pebble," he smiled at her. He held the pebble above the sink and let it drop to the water. It formed ripple after ripple and they watched in silence for more than a minute until the water was finally still again.

"One perfect pebble can continue to affect the water long after it is gone. If you think of those ripples as the fond memories that others hold, than this special pebble has a gentle but stronger affect on life than the big one. It leaves a void that will be noticed. A gentle ebbing that soothes so many. It will be missed much longer than the one that made the big splash," he said as he continued to look in the sink.

"Where do you come up with these analogies?" Mary asked, shaking her head.

"It's not original. My grandfather gave me a similar demonstration one time years ago when we were fishing together," Brian told her.

"Well he left his own ripple, because it has just washed over me," Mary contemplated.

Brian let the water drain from the sink and turned to Mary who was drying the pebbles.

"Brad was doing so well this year. Christmas would have been really great for them. They wouldn't have needed any help at all," Brian said to Mary.

"I know," Mary answered.

"I guess there's another way to look at it," Brian continued, "Brad had been doing well all year, so in some respects it was probably the best ten months of their marriage. They were really enjoying themselves here."

"True," said Mary, "and in a place like this, they are truly missed by so many. If they had been somewhere down south, fewer people would have felt the loss. Their ripple will be longer lasting here."

"You're lucky Mary," smiled Brian.

"Why's that?" she asked.

"When you die, so many people will feel the void," he answered.

Mary looked at Brian for a moment. She wasn't sure if he was being serious or sarcastic. He could have his caustic moments and she was afraid that he had misinterpreted her comments about a small town. She was relieved when he smiled.

"I'm serious," he continued, "That's what life is all about! How many people are touched or affected by your death. If nobody notices when you die, it hasn't been much of a life has it?"

"I guess not," Mary answered thoughtfully.

"A life is measured by how many people truly agonize at your death," Brian murmured, "It has to be a life worth dying for."

"Ironic, but true," answered Mary.

"It's Christmas! Let's blow this pop stand!" Brian grabbed her hand and pulled her out into the cold evening.

Chapter Twenty-Three

The winter of '77 was severe. There wasn't much snow, but it was dark, cold and windy for the entire month of January. Every day was a trial in survival. Mary kept her spirits up by planning her evening baths. The only time she was truly warm that winter was in a steaming tub.

Boredom had set in with Brian and although he was reading a lot, Mary knew it wouldn't be long before he would be planning another prank. The long, cold winter evenings were very conducive to creative thought, and for Brian that usually included a practical joke of some kind.

Brian was sitting by the fireplace with a new book when Mary came out of the bedroom. She had been getting ready for the last Saturday night of January. They were meeting everyone at the hotel for dinner and drinks.

"Fire looks nice tonight," observed Mary.

"Yea, it does. But I'll tell you, I still think somebody is taking some of our wood," he answered, "When I went out there earlier, the pile looked smaller than it should."

"Well it would, wouldn't it? This is the coldest winter yet. We've lit a fire almost every night. I don't think we built so many last year," said Mary.

"Maybe you're right, but it looks highly suspicious to me!" responded Brian, raising one eyebrow and attempting to look very detective-like.

"And I wish you'd stop telling people that you think someone is stealing our wood. That's a serious complaint in a small town!" Mary chided.

"You're right, you're right. It's just that it is so cold and the woodpile is going down fast. I want to be able to have a fire all winter," answered Brian.

At that moment there was a quiet knock at the door; more of a little tap than a knock. For a moment, neither of them was sure if someone was actually at the door or if the wind was making sounds. Mary went to check. When she opened the door there was Eddie. He quickly slipped inside and shut the door silently.

"Hi guys. I was just passing by on my way to the hotel when I saw something at the side of your house. So I went around, came back and slipped into your driveway as quietly as I could. I think there's an animal near your woodpile," he almost whispered.

Brian jumped up and they all went to the side window to look out. Brian turned off the living room lights so they could see outside more clearly. There, beside the woodpile, was something large and dark moving about. Eddie asked Mary for a flashlight, and Brian grabbed his baseball bat. He threw on his parka and he and Eddie walked slowly around the back of the house. Mary stayed inside at the window watching.

It seemed like an eternity before she saw the beam from the flashlight round the corner of the house. The large intruder was still walking slowly around the yard near the woodpile. Then she saw Eddie leading the way and Brian creeping up behind him, bat in hand. Suddenly the creature leaped at Eddie, Brian screamed and stepped back, raising the bat. Eddie isn't keeping the light on the animal very well, she was thinking. Eddie moved a little to the right, keeping the beam low to the ground. The creature leapt at Brian. Mary gasped with fright. Then suddenly the fur flew off its body and there stood Pedley yelling 'boo'. She could hear Eddie and Jackson laughing hysterically and Brian shouting to them that they were idiots. She shook her head and went to pour some drinks.

When the three men came back and opened the front door, it was far from a quiet entrance.

"What the hell were you doing out there?" Brian was asking.

"I was just doing my job!" Jackson answered.

"And what exactly does that mean?" continued Brian.

"Well, you've been complaining that someone is stealing your wood. So I was working undercover . . . as a woodchuck." Jackson and Eddie roared with laughter again. Mary joined in.

"I'm surrounded by idiots!" exclaimed Brian.

"True, true, but very funny idiots," laughed Mary.

"I might have killed you with the baseball bat!" Brian said to Jackson.

"I think you would have pissed your pants long before you ever thought of swinging the bat," laughed Pedley.

"What am I going to do without you?" Brian chuckled.

"I'm not gone yet. You've got five more months of entertainment and pleasure before I depart for the sunny coast," answered Jackson.

They finished their drinks, laughing and recounting the woodchuck event several times, before heading off to the hotel to join the others.

Bob and Sandra, Jim and his wife, were waiting for them when they arrived. Of course, all four were in on the plot and were anxious to hear how the scene had played out. Brian loved to play tricks on others, but he also truly enjoyed a good prank coming from chums. He had once told Mary that when friends take the time to carry out an elaborate caper, it was one way of saying how much they cared for you.

Father O'Reilly joined them just as Eddie and Jackson were about to tell the woodchuck tale. Bob and Jim were gasping for breath by the time the pair had finished. Brian and Mary had also added colourful descriptors as the event was recounted.

"By the way Brian, your woodpile will be back to its original size tomorrow afternoon," laughed Bob.

"I knew it!" yelled Brian, "You guys have been stealing my wood!"

"Only so you would complain, and I could go undercover!" laughed Jackson.

"You fellows and your shenanigans!" Father chuckled, "Never a dull moment in this town."

"How much wood, could a woodchuck chuck, if a woodchuck could chuck wood?" chanted Eddie.

That set the entire group off for the next hour trying to create new tongue-twisters. Bob even had to go and get pads and pencils for everyone. It started as simple entertainment, progressed to a serious level, with dictionaries brought to the table, and ended as a competition. The evening climaxed, with each one of the group reciting the tongue-twister that they had created and the others in the bar casting ballots for the best recitation. It was a good night. Things were back to normal again. Time had begun to heal the pain and resentment caused by the cabin fire. It would never be forgotten, but it was time to laugh again.

Mary had leaned over to Father O'Reilly and whispered to him how nice it was to hear some real laughter again. He turned to her and said, "To everything there is a season, and a time to every purpose under the heaven."

"A time to weep, and a time to laugh. I know that song Father. Pete Seeger, 1952," said Mary.

"Oh it's much older than that my love. Ecclesiastes 3," responded Father with a smile.

"Don't I feel foolish!" chuckled Mary.

"It's a good book! You should read it sometime," smiled Father.

"Maybe I will!" answered Mary.

Chapter Twenty-Four

Mary was woken abruptly the next morning. Brian was yelling at her to get up immediately. She jumped out of bed and saw Brian running out to start the truck. He called to her to throw on some clothes fast. There was no time for questions. She knew something was wrong.

When Brian came back in the house he took off his parka. He was still in his pyjamas and ran to the bedroom to change. Mary was dressed and washing her face at the bathroom sink.

"What's happening?" she called to Brian.

"Come on, we can talk in the truck," he answered.

They hopped into Brian's truck. It was still freezing in the cab as they pulled out of the driveway.

"What's so important?" Mary asked.

"Someone called from the cottage hospital. There's been a serious accident a few miles south, and some guy is in bad shape. The medical evacuation plane is flying in to pick him up. He's lost a lot of blood and they need you. We're supposed to meet them at the airport," he explained.

"Good Lord! I've given lots of blood over the years, but never directly to a particular person. It must be really serious," murmured Mary while she looked out the side window.

Mary had been donating blood every three months since her eighteenth birthday. She was a 'universal donor'. Her blood type was O Negative. The irony of blood types is that anyone can receive O Negative in a dire emergency, but O Negative blood types can only receive O Negative.

There was no blood bank in Everet. The cottage hospital delivered babies; otherwise it operated more as a clinic. If anyone required surgery they planned for it in Whitehorse or down south. The hospital doctor kept a record of blood types for emergencies. When she had moved to Everet, the doctor had told her that she was the youngest and healthiest person in town with O Negative blood. He had asked her if she would mind donating in time of emergency and she had agreed without hesitation. It was just one of those things you do without thinking that it will ever really be necessary.

They drove the rest of the way in silence. They were both still half asleep as Brian veered into the airport and onto the tarmac. They jumped out of the truck and ran over to the local ambulance which was already waiting on the runway. One of the Everet nurses greeted them. The doctor was inside the ambulance with the patient. She explained that the victim was a man in his thirties. There was severe damage to his right leg and he had lost a lot of blood. The doctor suspected some additional internal bleeding and he believed that the man would not last the flight to Whitehorse without a transfusion.

While the nurse spoke she was taking Mary's finger and pricking it for a small blood sample. She explained that she needed to check some basics and ensure that Mary was healthy enough to donate.

"I haven't eaten breakfast, but I had a big dinner last night. I haven't been sick for months. I'll be fine," explained Mary.

"We need to begin right away," said the nurse, "Brian come stand over here I'll need you to hold the bag." She handed Brian the plastic bag that would hold Mary's blood.

Mary sat on the bumper of the ambulance and slipped her parka off one arm. The nurse prepared Mary's arm, gently slid in the needle and taped it in place. Then she went back to help the doctor inside the ambulance. Brian sat down beside Mary holding the bag low between his knees.

"Well, good morning!" he smiled at Mary. "You okay?"

"Sure," she smiled back.

As they were speaking, the medi-evac plane was heard in the distance. In moments it was circling overhead. The ambulance driver and a couple of airport staff came from the small terminal and waved the plane in.

"Can you come with us?" the nurse asked Brian.

"No problem," replied Brian and he tossed his truck keys to one of the airport staff.

Brian and Mary boarded the plane first and then the others helped move the patient on board. It was then that Mary realized there was also a woman walking beside the stretcher and holding the man's hand. She looked shaken and bruised.

By the time everyone was on board, Mary's blood bag was half full. The doctor greeted them with a smile and a nod then explained that the patient needed the blood immediately. They took the first bag and replaced it with a new, empty one. As Mary's blood began to flow again, she watched as her first bag emptied into the dying man. No one spoke except the medical team as they monitored the patient.

"Mary," began the doctor, "he needs more than a pint. Although a pint is the normal donation, it's safe to give two pints. You may feel a little weak, but he needs it."

"Of course," whispered Mary.

It wasn't until the third half pint was entering the man's body that the doctor said, "There! He's stabilizing."

"How are you doing Mary?" he continued, "Do you think you can complete the last half pint?"

"I'm feeling fine," said Mary, "I feel foolish that you're even asking about me!"

"Just make sure you have a good meal after this, preferably some liver," the doctor advised. "She may feel faint Brian. Stay close and keep an eye on her."

Brian nodded. Both he and Mary were a little overwhelmed with the proceedings. They landed in Whitehorse as the needle was being removed from Mary's arm. The last of her blood was attached to the recipient as they moved him off the plane to the ambulance and medical team waiting on the runway. The young woman glanced up at Mary and nodded through glassy eyes. Mary returned the nod and closed her eyes.

"We'll just refuel and wait for the doctors to confer then we'll get you back to Everet," the pilot told them as he was stepping from the plane, "I'll bring you back some food and drink."

Mary and Brian were alone. Brian let out a long, deep sigh and put his arm around Mary. She leaned against him and closed her eyes again.

"Talk about the 'gift of life'! You can't get any more hands on than this!" Brian whispered in her ear.

Mary didn't answer. Her mind was bouncing between the patient, the woman, her blood and Father's O'Reilly's quote the night before; a time for every purpose under heaven. It was a spiritual moment of sorts. That's what maturing is all about, she was thinking, realizing how quickly things can change from good to desperate, from happiness to pain. When you're young, you think that you're immortal. As you become wiser with age, you learn to appreciate the good times because you've experienced some bad times. She promised herself that she would work harder to appreciate every moment of every day.

"My God life can be tough up here," Mary commented, "so many crises!"

"Not really. Not when you think about a big city and the sirens blaring all day and night. The difference is that down there you don't know everyone. An ambulance or a fire engine blazes by, but you don't think about it graphically. Up here the contact is more direct. We see the emergency and we feel the tragedy."

"Mmmm . . . well I've had enough for one winter!" answered Mary, "I hope he makes it."

They were back in Everet by mid-afternoon. Brian ran to get the truck and then helped Mary off the plane. She felt fine. As they drove into town, he suggested that they stop at the hotel restaurant and have some liver. Mary agreed that it was probably a good idea.

V

The Dangers of Green Chartreuse and Testosterone

Chapter Twenty-Five

*P*eople living north of sixty spend most of the year working and saving toward a winter holiday. It is the ultimate reward to fly out in sub-zero temperatures and arrive on a tropical island within twenty four hours. Brian and Mary were no different. They had been preoccupied with images of Hawaii since Christmas Day. Bob and Sandra had booked flights for the same week in March. They would all be staying at the same hotel on the island of Maui.

As soon as Brian had decided to purchase the airline tickets as a Christmas present for Mary, he had given Bob the flight details. Memories of the winter vacation were something to savour for months after the return. It was more enjoyable to be reminiscing with friends than boring others with your photos and stories.

It would be an eight-day excursion. Mary only had a week off school. Bob and Sandra could not leave the hotel for more than a short period at a time, so eight days suited them fine. They would fly out on a Saturday and return the following Saturday. Each Saturday would be spent in the air, which meant they had only six days to achieve the ultimate goal of any winter vacation, the tan.

People would talk of the relaxation, the golf games and the evening dinners, but returning from a tropical winter retreat without a golden suntan would mystify any Arctic dweller. It was the only souvenir worth considering. Walking in to work the day after a return flight, several shades darker than anyone else on staff was all that really mattered. The tan was the tangible proof that you had truly been to the tropics.

Mary and Sandra knew that six days would not afford them a very deep tan. If they rushed into the sun too quickly they would burn and peel for the entire week. So they had each ordered a sunlamp. The plan was to begin using the lamps each day for ten or fifteen minutes, so they would have a base tan before departure.

The lamps arrived two weeks before the Spring break. The instructions were read carefully and schedules devised to afford maximum results. It was decided that the upper body was of top priority. After all, once they returned, they would be covered again in winter clothing. Leg tan was of little importance. This pre-tanning plan was no secret. Everyone in the north understood the value placed on the vacation suntan. Sunlamps were relatively new to the market and not many people had used them yet. Everyone was interested to see the results of the two week pre-vacation tanning sessions.

The two couples knew that the lamps were powerful and demanded respect. A few years ago they had held a birthday party for Jackson. They had decided to make it a Hawaiian theme party. Bob and Sandra had transformed their house into a beach resort. They had filled the bathtub with water and added massive amounts of blue and green food colouring, so it could serve as the hotel pool. Two sunlamps had been strategically placed in the living room, along with lounge chairs and beach towels. Everyone had arrived in bathing suits, or summer wear.

It had been a great party. It was the next morning that the pain set in. Almost everyone had severe sunburns. No one had realized the power of sunlamps. It had not been a pleasant experience. Jackson had peeling skin for a week. Eddie could not sit properly for days because his upper legs were burnt so badly. A month later it was a big joke, but the few days following the party were not very funny. Since then, everyone had developed a great respect for the sunlamp and its potential to injure. As a result of this group experience, the two couples planned to use the sunlamps sparingly and to follow the enclosed instructions carefully. No one wanted a repeat of the Pedley birthday party fiasco.

Mary had set up an area in the living room for tanning. The sunlamp sat on a small table about two feet off the floor. A large towel was placed on the carpet. She had drawn up a daily schedule for each of them to follow. They would begin with ten minutes on each side for the first few days. Brian was not too enthused about the idea, but smiled and kept his mouth shut. He had learned to choose his battles wisely, and so the sun tanning sessions did not become an issue. Unfortunately, something else occurred that would upset the equilibrium and throw Brian off balance.

There was a mining town about one hundred miles east of Everet. It had a population twice the size of Everet, but there was almost no contact between the two communities. Mining towns were virtually self-sufficient. They had their own airstrip and so residents were flown in and out with company planes. The facilities were magnificent and in most cases employees did not have any reason to leave the comfort of the company town. It was a completely different experience than life in Everet. The mine employees had no personal commitment to the north. Most of them owned homes in the south, and had personal goals completely unrelated to the land that they currently inhabited. The mine could have been located anywhere. It sat in its own little bubble.

But on the Saturday preceding the Hawaiian vacation, Everet was invaded by miners! It was not actually an invasion, more of a visit, but it was difficult for Brian to view it in that light. He had walked in to the hotel to have a drink with Bob and wait for Mary to finish her tanning session and join them. As he entered the front door of the establishment, he was surprised to hear a great deal of noise coming from the bar. It usually didn't liven up until later in the evening. Bob met him in the lobby and asked if he could come and carry some cases of beer into the bar. A few guys from the mining town had been out on a winter excursion and were stopping overnight on their way home.

Brian helped Bob restock the bar and then they sat down for a drink. Brian was always happy to see new faces and meet new people. He had not seen the arrival of these men as any type of threat until Mary joined them an hour later. As soon as she entered the bar, the mood changed. The glances, the nods and whispers of the visitors made Brian sit up and begin to posture slightly. Later Bob would refer to the evening as 'the invasion of the men in heat'. Brian saw no humour in the tale. His territory was being threatened. This was serious!

It is amazing how a little competition makes men sit up and take notice of their partners. Brian was suddenly very interested in Mary's attire. He asked if the jeans she had on were new. No they were not. He asked if she was chilly in the slinky blouse that she was wearing. No she was not. He made the mistake of asking if her jeans were fitting a little more tightly than usual. Mary was not impressed with this observation and told Brian to go to hell. Bob smiled and sat back to enjoy the jousting. Meanwhile, the miners had sent a round of drinks to their table. Bob hollered a thank you. Mary nodded to them and raised her glass. Brian sulked.

By eight o'clock the bar was packed. Jackson and Eddie had joined their friends. It was turning into a good evening for everyone except Brian. Mary was becoming more beautiful with each drink. He was sitting beside her and when Jackson had tried to pull up a chair and sit between them, Brian had slid closer to Mary and told Pedley to sit somewhere else. No one had noticed the dynamics of the room except Bob. It was his job to pay close attention to the mood in the bar, but he was also enjoying the silent sparring between the young men. "Biology," he thought, "some things never change. Brian will be pissing in every corner of the room soon. I'd better keep an eye on things."

The men from the mining town were actually not miners at all. Although they were all in simple blue jeans and shirts, it was obvious that they were upper management. They were polite and well spoken, but it was their hands that made the statement. They were not the hands of miners or working men. There was no hint of grime or damage. These were hands that worked with paper, not oil and rock. As far as Bob was concerned, this made things even more interesting. It would be an evening of battle, but it would be brain and not brawn planning the strategy.

Mary was oblivious to the potential crisis. Her mind was on Hawaii. She had no idea that

Brian was in possession mode and felt an imminent threat close by. Pedley had picked up on the vibes, but the visitors were minding their own business. It was really an innocent scene, but things are magnified in small, isolated towns. Brian was not accustomed to competition. Saturday nights were more like family gatherings than nights on the town. All his senses had been fired up and he was on some sort of primitive invasion alert. Unfortunately the bar did not close for another four hours. It was going to be a long night for Brian.

Chapter Twenty-Six

They were still chatting about Hawaii. Eddie was telling them about a good restaurant that he and his wife had enjoyed on their last trip. Brian was beginning to relax and worry less about the new men in town.

"There's a little restaurant down the beach from our hotel that has a couple a tables on the sand. It's supposed to be wonderful to dine there at sunset," said Mary.

"That sounds nice. Did you see it in a brochure?" asked Brian.

"No. One of the guys from out of town told me about it," answered Mary as she nodded towards the enemy table.

"When were you talking to them?" questioned Brian.

Mary looked at Brian curiously and asked him how much he'd had to drink. She said that one fellow from the table of miners had come over a couple of times to talk with them. Had Brian not noticed? Brian sat up and the adrenalin began to flow again. He had not seen any of the strangers at their table. The conversation about restaurants had continued, but Brian was not listening.

"Which guy has come over to our table? Brian asked Pedley.

"The good-looking one in the green, plaid shirt," Jackson was trying to keep a straight face.

"I haven't seen him come over here. Am I blind?" continued Brian.

"Actually, I think you were taking a piss every time he came over."

"The sneaky son of a bitch," thought Brian. "He waits until I'm out of the room to prey on my woman. That's it! No more washroom trips this evening. I've got to stay put right beside her."

Although no washroom trip was a simple solution to his dilemma, it was an impossible proposition. Brian tried sipping his drink, but then he would forget and take a big gulp. It wasn't long before his bladder was bursting. He got up and literally ran to the washroom. He was back in seconds with his arm around Mary again.

"Did we have any visitors while I was gone?" he asked Pedley.

"Gone where?" queried Jackson, "Did you go out of town this week?"

"No! I mean just now when I went to the washroom. Did anyone come over to our table?" Brian whispered.

"I don't think so," answered Jackson.

"What kind of a police officer are you? You should know everything that is going on at any given time!" responded Brian.

"I know everyone in the room and I know that everyone is having a good time. I don't think I have to monitor the movements of every individual in the bar!" laughed Pedley.

"You don't know those guys," said Brian as he looked towards the table of miners.

"I know where they came from, and I know where they're going. They look like a bunch of very normal guys and they are minding their own business." What else do I need to know?" answered Pedley.

"But what are their motives?" asked Brian.

"What the hell are you talking about?" grimaced Pedley. "They're having a beer and a good night's sleep before they head off home tomorrow. Pretty basic motives if you ask me!"

Brian gave up. No one would understand how he was feeling. No one else was even paying attention to the table of strangers. Brian knew that at least one of them was making a play for Mary. He was not going to be fooled into believing it was innocent. It was no coincidence that the man in the green plaid shirt had only come over to talk to his woman when he had gone to the washroom. He glared across the room at the enemy. Eye contact was made between the two men, and the man in question raised his glass in a mock toast to Brian and nodded with a smile.

"Okay." thought Brian, "Now he knows that I know. He'd better stay clear of this table if he knows what's good for him!" and Brian straightened his back and slid a little closer to Mary.

Bob was actually monitoring the situation much more closely than the police, as the evening progressed. He had been operating the hotel for more than a decade and he recognized the potential for problems more quickly than the young officer. He used to laugh with Sandra and tell her that it was not the booze that actually caused fights in a bar. Men and booze were fine. It was men and booze, with women thrown into the equation which caused all the tension. He wasn't too worried about the dynamics of the room this evening. Mary was not a trucker's girlfriend. In other words, she was not flirtatious and she did not see jealousy as some distorted sign of love from her mate. She was unaware of the glances and toasts occurring around her. There were no coy little smiles coming from her. She was not trying to raise the temperature in the room as some women do. She honestly had not noticed Brian's increased attention. In her mind it was just another Saturday night in Everet.

Meanwhile, Brian was in defence mode. It was not totally a figment of his imagination. The green plaid man was responding to his glares with a knowing smile, and of course the more Brian drank, the braver he became. The deep-rooted chivalry DNA was rising to the surface. He would protect his woman and his territory.

He would stand tall as the smartest and bravest knight of the realm.

Suddenly the room was full of gasps, as the barmaid walked to the miners' table with a tray of flaming drinks. The men were having a good time, toasting each other and gliding their hands through the flame on each glass.

"What are they drinking over there?" asked Jackson.

"Green Chartreuse," answered Bob. "Burns beautifully, but tastes like turpentine. They'll be sorry in the morning."

"I haven't touched that shit for years," added Eddie. "I had a hangover for days the last time I drank it."

Brian was not listening. All his attention was focused on the green plaid man and the green Chartreuse. He felt as if the dual had begun. The gauntlet dropped and the weapon chosen. "Fine with me," he thought, "I accept the challenge. Flaming drinks it is then!"

Brian rose and sauntered over to the bar. He knew instinctively that he must make a point of rising to request the drinks. In order to remain in a position of pride and power, he felt that he had to strut around the room. He had to appear to be confident and in total control of his territory. Bob kept an eye on the posturing and postulating. It was still innocent enough. The funniest aspect so far was that Mary was totally oblivious to the antics of her war hero. She had no idea that he was preparing for battle.

Brian casually called for a round of flaming green Chartreuse and slowly returned to his friends. He made sure that he stopped at every table along the way to talk and joke with the patrons. He was shaking hands and slapping people on the back as he meandered slowly toward Mary. He looked like a politician out on the hustings. It was his way of pointing out that he was on home ground, surrounded by friends. He was setting the borders and boundaries.

The two girls working the evening shift in the bar were busy. They were trying to keep all the guests content and watered, while they prepared twelve more flaming green Chartreuse. The miners, as well as Brian, had ordered rounds for their respective tables. With drinks such as these, the presentation was very important. When they were all poured and set on fire, each girl took a tray to a table. This way, neither group would feel slighted. "The tacit knowledge of a good barmaid is a valuable skill." thought Bob.

By this point in the evening, everyone had drunk more than enough. Eddie had not stuck a straw in each of his ears yet, so he was still lucid enough to decline the flaming poison. Jackson was curiously turning the small liqueur glass and asking Bob for details on alcoholic percentage. Mary had raised her glass to have a closer look at the flame. Sandra bumped her arm by mistake and the green liquid spilled all over the table. There was a small commotion as tiny flames danced around the other glasses. Brian took some napkins and doused the fire as he kept his eyes on green plaid man. The miners were showing off by carefully tipping the burning drinks into their mouths and hold the flames on their tongues. Then opening and closing their lips. Each time they opened their mouths, the flames would dance out. It was quite impressive and they had captured the attention of everyone in the room.

Brian rested his elbows on the table and placed both hands over his nose in prayer formation. Then he parted his hands and rubbed a hand over each cheek. He ran his fingers through his hair. He was ready to demonstrate that he too could hold a flame on his tongue and entertain a crowd. He was unaware that he had just spread the alcohol from Mary's drink all over his face and head. He raised his flaming glass and toasted green plaid man, smiling snidely. He took a large sip and turned to Mary to stick out his tongue which held the small flame. In a flash, the flames crept up his cheeks. Spontaneously his eyebrows caught on fire and then his entire head of hair. Everyone was caught off guard. Time stood still as Brian went up in flames. It was Bob who had the wherewithal to holler at the barmaids for a fresh towel. One of the girls raced over with the rag and Bob smothered the flames. Silence fell on the room.

Brian may have been able to save face if everyone had started to laugh, but much to his horror he was suddenly surrounded by sympathy and concern. Everyone was taking this much too seriously and he felt like an idiot. Then out of nowhere green plaid man appeared.

"Are you okay buddy?" he asked, "I'm a doctor. Let me take a look."

"Oh this is just great," thought Brian. "I'm an asshole and he's a fucking doctor!"

"You've got some minor burns. It's going to hurt like hell for a few days, but it's nothing serious. You should probably go over to the hospital and let them clean it up so you don't get an infection. But you'll be fine in a couple of days," counselled the smiling doctor.

"Jesus Christ you stink!" said Eddie, "Nothing like the smell of burning hair."

"What were you thinking?" asked Mary.

Great! Now he was going to be publicly reprimanded by Mary in front of green plaid man. There was only one option and that was to retreat quickly and quietly, before he was totally humiliated in the presence of the enemy troops. He leaned over and told Mary that he would meet her at home. He asked Pedley to take him to the hospital. They left the hotel, but Brian could hear the laughter return to the bar before the front door of the hotel closed behind them.

Chapter Twenty-Seven

When he returned from the cottage hospital Brian went straight to bed. He did not sleep well. The doctor had given him some wonderful swabs that alleviated the pain from the burns, but if anything touched his face it was excruciating. He normally slept on his stomach, but he had to sleep on his back so his face was not touching anything. Every time he dozed off, he would forget about the burns on his eyebrows and forehead. He would roll on to his side or wipe an arm across his face and the pain would wake him up. He had to keep his distance from Mary. There was no way to cuddle with her without putting his face in danger, so he lay on the far side of the bed. Every time Mary would roll over or change position he would tense up and go on high alert. The doctor and nurse at the hospital had been helpful and professional in their treatment, but Brian had found their behaviour annoying. Jackson had entertained them with the story of the green Chartreuse and the flaming shot glasses. They had asked for more details and numerous retellings of the spontaneous combustion moment far too many times. Brian had a burned face and a bruised ego. He did not need to hear the tale over and over again. Jackson was oblivious to Brian's mood and had a fine time amusing the hospital staff.

It is interesting how people create their own reality based on their own perceptions. Jackson saw the event as Brian once again dominating the evening and entertaining everyone, albeit this time to the extreme. Brian saw the evening as a total disaster, embarrassing and humiliating to the extreme. When they spoke to each other about the scene, they were actually each speaking about a totally different experience. Jackson laughed at Brian's responses and was impressed with his friend's dry wit and sarcasm. Brian was annoyed at Pedley's redundant harping and wished that he would stop enjoying his pain and suffering quite so much.

So when they parted in front of Brian's door, Jackson had driven off with a honk and a smile, while Brian had sulked into the house with a scowl. He spent about fifteen minutes in front of the bathroom mirror studying the damage to his face. His eyebrows were gone, except for a small tuft at the far end of each brow. It would look better without the remaining hair he thought, but when he tried to cut the hair it hurt too much and he had to give up. The area around his brows was very tender. His forehead was also bright red and burned. Even his nostrils were slightly damaged. The flames had shot straight up from his mouth, catching fire to his nose hairs, then his eyebrows and finally his forelocks. By the time Bob had doused the inferno, the blaze had destroyed all the hair in its path. They had travelled quickly and even above his forehead, sat a large patch of crinkled hair that resembled melted plastic. It was too painful to touch any area at the moment. He would have to live with the damage for a couple of days before trying to salvage his good looks.

Brian took one of the painkillers that the doctor had given him then carefully undressed and even more carefully positioned himself in bed next to Mary to try and get some sleep. He spent most of the night thinking about the next day and how he could recover some self-respect. As with many people in an awkward position, he decided that the best defence was an offence. So by early morning he had edited the events of the preceding evening into a version that suited his view of the world and would enhance his self-esteem. By the time he got out of bed, he believed it.

He put on the coffee and carefully showered. He got dressed and dabbed his face once more with the miracle swabs from the doctor. Whatever the wipes contained took away the pain for about thirty minutes. By the time he had finished, Mary was up and having her first sip of coffee.

She smiled as Brian entered the kitchen. Then she gasped in horror.

"Brian! You left so quickly last night that I didn't realize how much of your face you had burned!"

"Yes, it was quite the wildfire! But it certainly livened up the evening, didn't it?"

"I guess so. Was that the purpose, to spark up the conversation? Excuse the pun."

"Of course! Anything for a laugh." Brian poured another coffee.

"You're not telling me that you purposely lit your face on fire!"

"No. I'm telling you that I created an opportunity that would lead to some type of memorable event, regardless of the outcome!"

"Whatever that means! Does it hurt?"

"Actually no. Not unless I touch it."

"Well it looks bizarre!" Mary moved closer to study the damage in detail.

"Thank you very much. Then the desired effect has been achieved!"

"I think perhaps you are certifiably insane. Although now that I know you're okay, in the light of day, looking back, it certainly was funny! Maybe I'm crazy too."

Brian was pleased. His approach had worked. Mary was laughing with him rather than at him. He was in control of the situation again. It was of the utmost importance that he manage to turn this disaster into another great 'Brian antic'; another story to enhance his immortality. If he continued with this attitude for the rest of the day, he would be Brian the Hysterical instead of Brian the Loser.

He did not realize that everyone who had been at his table already viewed it as such, with the exception of Bob who knew exactly what had been transpiring throughout the evening. Bob was confident that Brian would somehow turn the tables and save face, and he had no intention of publicly castrating his friend. He loved to watch people like Brian interact socially. It was a true art form to be able to entertain others. It was a craft he had practiced for years and people like Brian gave him a great deal of material to rework and embellish. He was looking forward to seeing Brian and Mary later in the day and to listen to Brian recount the green Chartreuse tale. "I wonder if he'll even mention the miners," Bob chuckled to himself, "It would be best if he dwelled on the liqueur rather than the testosterone duel that triggered the event."

After Mary lay for ten minutes under the sunlamp, she and Brian drove to the hotel for Sunday brunch. The Everet Inn offered a nice buffet on Sundays. Usually everyone met around two o'clock to enjoy the meal and recharge themselves for another week of work and cold weather. Bob, Sandra and Father O'Reilly were already eating salad when the couple arrived. Jackson and Eddie came in shortly thereafter, complaining of the icy wind and their hangovers.

"I don't have a hangover," Brian told them, "It must be the painkillers that the doctor gave me."

"Well that's the answer!" continued Eddie, "Every Saturday night at midnight, we go to the hospital for medication before we go home!"

The conversation swung between mediocre chit chat and swelling descriptions of the green Chartreuse flames as well as Brian's grand finale. Brian managed to remain the star of the story. He was enjoying the attention when Bob disrupted his mood.

"Oh by the way, the fellas from the mine left this morning, but the doctor left a note for you, Mary," Bob pulled a paper from his shirt pocket.

No one thought much of it except Brian who stiffened in his seat and sat up attentively. He looked over Mary's shoulder to read the message.

"Isn't that nice of him! It's the name of the restaurant on the beach in Maui. He says that he remembered the name late last night and wanted to make sure that we had it for our trip."

Brian sat back with a sneer but managed to keep his mouth shut. Bob smiled and kept quiet also. The rest of the group were saying how considerate and thoughtful it was of the stranger to leave the note.

"It also says that he hopes you are feeling okay this morning and that your burns shouldn't hurt for too long," continued Mary.

"Hmmpp," Brian straightened and crossed his arms, "Out-of-towners never understand our humour!"

"Poor guys! Not everyone can be as cool as we are. It must be hard on them to watch us without envy!" Jackson sat back and puffed out his chest.

"Concern for someone whose face went up in flames is perfectly normal," Mary defended, "Especially from a doctor!"

"It really was a towering inferno," Eddie was cracking a raw egg to drop in his tomato juice, his favourite hangover cure. "It looked more like a scene from a cartoon than real life!"

"I thought it was much more realistic, more like a good movie," Father O'Reilly was studying Eddie's concoction with horror.

"I guess so!" Eddie threw back the morning cocktail in one gulp. "It was real, Father!"

"The look on your face through the flames!" Jackson sputtered as he choked on his coffee.

The replay of the previous evening began again. Everyone was enjoying themselves immensely, especially Brian. Good friends, good conversation, good stories. It was another great Sunday afternoon in Everet. Brian looked around the table and smiled. Life was good except for one thing . . . he needed more of the miracle wipes from the hospital.

Chapter Twenty-Eight

*B*rian's face went through a series of evolutionary changes over the next week. By the time the two couples were departing for the sunny south, it looked quite awful. There were several variations of colour, in scattered blotches from his hairline down to his upper lip. The tenderness as well as the redness had gone, but what was left looked like unruly permanent birthmarks. At the airport people would glance and then quickly look away, so as not to be caught staring.

Bob and Brian were sitting in a Vancouver Airport lounge while Sandra and Mary were on a spending spree through the duty free area. Excepting the few shops in Whitehorse and the worn out Sears catalogue, they had not been shopping for more than a year. They knew that they should wait until their arrival in Hawaii, but the urge was uncontrollable. They started out with the good intention of just looking, but it was more than either woman could handle. By the time they joined the men, their arms were full of various bags and boxes.

"I thought duty free was too expensive and you were going to wait until we landed," Brian commented.

"I know, I know," answered Mary, "but we couldn't help ourselves!"

"Do we have enough money left to pay for the hotel?" Bob smiled at Sandra.

"It was a package deal, so our hotel is already paid for. Call it travel insurance."

A few minutes later their flight was called and they struggled off to their gate, bags in hand. As they boarded the plane and were putting everything into the overhead bins, Brian dramatically kissed his parka good bye, to the amusement of the other passengers.

Holiday flights are always special. Almost everyone on the flight was going to Hawaii for rest and relaxation, leaving behind the Canadian winter. There was a party atmosphere in the cabin. After takeoff Brian was wandering up and down the aisle, chatting with other passengers. By the time they were preparing to land, he knew everyone in proximity by first name. "It must be wonderful to truly love people so much," thought Mary, "I don't know where he gets the energy. Sometimes I wish that I could tap into his enthusiasm and lighten up. On the other hand, if we were both so fired up all the time, we'd drive all of our friends crazy. I'll write the postcards and let him meet everyone on the beach!"

When they landed in Honolulu and walked down the portable stairs from the plane, the heat hit them like a brick wall. Hawaiian girls put the traditional floral leis on each of them and of course Brian had to have a little dance on the tarmac. Then they went for a drink while they waited to connect to the smaller plane that would take them to Maui. By the time they arrived at the hotel on the outer island, they were exhausted, but too excited to sleep. They agreed to shower and change and meet in the lobby in an hour.

There is no moment quite as wonderful as the first hour of a winter vacation; sitting on an open lanai lounge or in a street café and savouring the new aromas and the warm night breeze. The four northerners were silent as they took a sip from their first fruit cocktails. The moment was fleeting. Suddenly out of nowhere twenty or thirty small motorbikes drove straight into the bar. Patrons all grabbed for their cocktails and frantically held on to each other. The bikers drove in and out among tables. They were obviously all intoxicated. They were not driving at deadly speeds, but they had tipped over a few tables and bumped a number of chairs.

"Don't worry hon, somebody will call the police if they don't disappear," Brian called to Mary above the noise of the engines.

"I doubt it!" hollered the man at the neighbouring table.

"Why not?" yelled Brian.

"Because these are cops! It's a police convention. They've been here for three long days. This is their last night. It'll get worse before it gets better," explained the guest. "I won't go on another vacation without asking first who is staying at the hotel!"

Bob smiled, "Well you know what they say. There's a thin line between a good cop and a good crook."

"Well then, these idiots must be fantastic cops!" noted a woman at another table.

"Listen, I'm way too sober for this, let's go back to our room and eat on the balcony," suggested Bob.

So the four new arrivals gingerly made their way to the lobby and then almost ran up to Bob and Sandra's room. They ordered a huge meal and Bob convinced the hotel to give them a discount on the room service explaining that they were virtual prisoners until the rowdy officers checked out. The room was on the second floor and overlooked the swimming pool. There were palm trees rising up on each side of the balcony and beautiful hibiscus bushes touching the balcony railings.

"This reminds me of Acapulco," Sandra picked a blossom and placed it tenderly behind Bob's ear. "Remember that hotel we stayed at near the cliffs?"

"Yea, you two should see the divers leap from the giant cliffs there. It's amazing!"

"Especially at night," Sandra was handing Mary and Brian each a blossom, "They hold torches in each hand. It's spectacular."

The group finished a couple of bottles of wine and moved on to a bottle of rye that Sandra had purchased at the duty free shop. The men were planning their first round of golf and the women were deciding what side of the pool would be best for the morning sun, when suddenly the peace was broken by the arrival of more drunken police officers. Several groups had descended on the pool area. It was interesting to watch the dissidents from a distance. Sandra and Mary rested their arms on the balcony railing and leaned over to get a better view of the revellers.

Mary and Brian's room was adjacent to Bob and Sandra's and the balconies joined. Brian stood up and hopped over the adjacent railing. He slid open the glass door to his room.

"Where are you going?" asked Mary turning around to look at Brian.

"To the can. Be back in a minute," he answered.

"It's a good job that we arrived late. Otherwise Brian wouldn't be able to stand it. He'd be down there with those guys in a flash."

Both Bob and Sandra nodded lazily.

Suddenly Bob looked past Mary, stood up and shouted, "What the hell are you doing?"

Mary and Sandra turned around to see Brian balancing on the balcony railing, holding a flaming roll of toilet paper high in each hand. Before anyone could react, he leaped off the balcony and dove into the pool. By the time he surfaced, the officers were all giving a standing ovation and yelling bravo. Mary fell back into her chair.

Bob was still standing and looking down at the pool.

"I think he's okay."

"That's too bad, because now I have to kill him!" simmered Mary.

"Mary! Mary!" came a voice from the pool below, "That was for you. Now we don't have to waste the money going to Mexico."

"Don't mention another place on earth while we're here, I don't want him pretending to be Evel Knievel tomorrow."

"Sandra my darling, remind me to get some rope and tie him to a palm tree in the morning."

Sandra held up her glass for a toast and said, "To a peaceful and relaxing week in the tropics."

"God help us!" added Mary.

Wisely and to his credit, Brian did not linger long at the pool. He accepted the accolades of the drunken audience and then went straight back up to his room. He snuggled into bed next to Mary and whispered in her ear.

"I couldn't help it Babe. As soon as Bob told the story of the divers in Acapulco the image just stuck in my mind. I couldn't get it out of my head."

"I know Brian. It's a terminal disease with you."

"More of a compulsive disorder I think."

"Well whatever it is, get a grip on it. I don't want to bury you and then sit around alone while I listen to Bob tell Brian stories for the next thirty years."

"I love you Mary Richardson!"

"Well try to find tamer ways to show me."

"How about right now?"

"I don't know Brian. I think you'll have trouble following the last act. That dive into the pool may have been the ultimate climax."

"My God, how stupid was that. I just upstaged myself!"

"Keep that in mind the next time you're hoping to get lucky," she giggled and rolled into his arms.

Chapter Twenty-Nine

The rest of the week passed all too quickly. It was filled with cycles of sunbathing and golfing, shopping and dining. By Friday night both Mary and Sandra had achieved golden tans. The men, on the other hand, had not worked as hard on any form of even colouration. Their backs were burned and peeling, their chests were white and their faces were various shades of brown and red. The sun had managed to exaggerate all the markings on Brian's face. Every damaged area had taken on a different hue.

They had decided to dine on the beach at the restaurant recommended by the doctor from the mining town. The table was facing the shore and the sun was preparing to set over the water. Sandra had asked one of the waiters to take a few snapshots of the four of them. As they posed for the camera, Bob put his arm around Sandra and said, "This may be the last time we need a winter vacation sweetheart." Sandra nodded and smiled.

"What do you mean?" asked Brian.

"We're putting the hotel up for sale. If we get a good offer then we're pulling up stakes and moving to Nevada."

"We're going to buy a little motel that we've had our eye on for years," continued Sandra.

"Ten rooms, a little bar and casino, and no restaurant! I've had my fill of the food industry! The work involved in preparing one sandwich and delivering it to a table equals five rounds in a bar. People rarely bitch about a rye and coke, but they'll complain for hours about one sandwich. Let someone else feed them!"

"And maybe you'll finally have the time to learn how to play chess!" said Sandra.

"My God! She's been after me to play chess with her since the day we met."

"It's a great game! I would like us to have something in common that we can enjoy together."

Mary was first to congratulate them. She went on about how much fun it would be to visit them. She asked about the temperatures year round. She wished them all the best and said that she'd keep her fingers crossed that they would get a great offer on the Everet Inn. Brian was not so pleased; first Jackson and now Bob. The place wouldn't be the same next winter with his two best friends gone.

"You're gonna leave me all alone with Eddie and Father O'Reilly!"

"Well actually we're leaving you alone with Eddie. Father O'Reilly just told me last week that he's being transferred to some settlement in the Eastern Arctic."

"You'll still have Jim," Sandra added.

"What about me?" blurted Mary, "You'll still have me!"

"I know, but you're my rock. I need some special pebbles around to keep me company."

"You'll find new pebbles," consoled Mary.

"What is this? Some kind of secret code you two speak?" queried Bob.

Bob continued, "It'll be like a semi-retirement for us. Slow down the pace a bit and have time to sit back and smell the roses, so to speak."

"Why does everyone talk so much about retirement?" exclaimed Brian. "Death is retirement. Eternal retirement! There's no need to slow down until God takes you!"

"I never thought of it that way. You sure do have a unique perspective on life, my man!" smiled Bob.

"It's the Protestant Work Ethic that was drilled into me since birth."

"It's not the Protestant Work Ethic!" Mary smiled and shook her head, "You're not motivated by your job and your duties to TranGas. You're motivated by practical jokes and socializing!"

"Okay then, it's the Ladley Play Ethic! It's the excitement that each morning brings, wondering what fantastic nonsense will avail itself to me before nightfall. If I didn't have this to look forward to each day, I'd be bored to death."

"How did you ever make it through school?" Mary ran her fingers through his hair.

"With kind teachers and a mother who understood me."

"Thank God for understanding mothers! Where would any of us be without our mothers?" pondered Bob.

"In jail!" quipped Brian.

The conversation moved on to the menu and the flight plans for the next day. They had to pack later that night, as their flight to Honolulu left at six in the morning. It would be depressing to take out the parkas and lay them on the sofa. The summer wear had to be packed up and blue jeans and flannel shirts prepared. At least it was almost the end of March. They would be returning to winter, but the sun would be shining and the snow would be sparkling. Spring was around the corner with new life and new plans for many of them.

Brian was unusually quiet on the return flights. Every time Mary would glance over at him, he would be staring out the window or sleeping against it. He even refused a couple of meals, which was very odd. Brian and Mary both loved airplane food. They were always fascinated by the organization of the tray and the way so much food was placed in such a small area. They had decided years ago that people who complained about airplane food were simply trying to act cool and cosmopolitan. By criticising the food on flights, it insinuated that one flew so often that the meals had become a bore. They would smile inwardly if they met someone who fit this mould and glance knowingly at each other. There was nothing pretentious about either Brian or Mary. They loved to sit next to someone who was experiencing their first flight and share in the curiosity and excitement. They were both very kind and sincerely enjoyed the company of others. They were also good listeners, which made them popular with their friends. They considered themselves as professional people watchers, so Mary was mystified by Brian's quiet demeanour on the trip home. New faces and situations always stimulated him, so it was really odd to watch him ignore the passengers and turn inward. "Perhaps we shouldn't take short winter vacations anymore," thought Mary. "The return to the real world is obviously too depressing for Brian.

The return to winter was not bothering Brian. It was the impending departure of so many friends that was depressing him. The last few years had been the best years of his adult life. He had found true joy in his eclectic mix of companions; a priest, a Mountie, an innkeeper, a mechanic and a gas fitter. They were all so different and yet they had found common ground in a small northern town. He had never considered the possibility that most everyone would eventually move on. He was sure that he would never find such a comfortable communion of friends again, and that had preoccupied his thoughts since early morning. He was not thinking of this winter at all, but of next winter and how lonely it was going to be without Jackson, Bob and Father O'Reilly.

He was going to have to make the most of the next few months. Time was running out for this amazing circle of souls. It was important to dwell on the here and now, and forget about the fork further down the road. It would come soon enough and he would have to deal with it eventually, but right now he had to start making plans for next weekend! Savour every moment and make as many memories as possible. This was his immediate game plan.

By the time they landed in Everet, Brian had confronted all his fears for the future and had joined Mary in conversation. They were all stiff and tired from the hours of travelling. The icy wind that greeted them as they left the warmth of the plane was harsh. They ran quickly into the airport. The men went out to start their trucks and then returned to the comfort of the small airport lobby to sit with their partners while the vehicles warmed up.

"Home sweet home!" groaned Bob.

After the plane refuelled and took off again, the airport staff came over and joined the two couples. Bob asked if all was well in town and if the hotel was still standing. There was general chit chat about the past week. Not much had happened while they were away. One of the staff asked about their vacation. Bob explained that it had been a quiet and relaxing week, except for the first evening when some lunatic had jumped from a balcony into the pool with a roll of flaming toilet paper in each hand.

"Why don't I ever see stuff like that?" asked one staff member.

"Because you don't travel with Brian!" responded Mary.

Chapter Thirty

"I'm gonna invite the guys over to play cards on Thursday night if that's all right with you," called Brian from the bathroom.

"No problem," said Mary as he joined her in the kitchen. "But wouldn't Friday night be better? Then you can sleep in on Saturday."

"From now on, the weekend begins on Thursday," answered Brian. "We only have a short time left before Jackson and Father O'Reilly leave. I've made some calculations, and if we start the weekend a day early from now on, then it turns into the equivalent of two extra weekends per month. So rather than twelve more weekends left, we actually have eighteen before they leave us."

"If you got together every night until June that would probably equal a year of weekends!"

"I thought of that already, but one of us would definitely die before spring thaw. We have to temper the farewell period with some common sense."

"Common sense! Don't tell me that you are actually reaching some early stage of maturity."

"I hope not!" Brian responded rather seriously. "Maturity is highly overrated. I think it's just an excuse boring people use to rationalize their dull existence."

"But can you gain wisdom without maturing?"

"Of course. Wisdom is when one knows what height of balcony to dive from. Maturity is never even considering the dive." He winked at her as he poured a coffee.

"Then you are wise beyond your years my love!" and she kissed him on his forehead. "Why don't I sleep at Sandra's and then Bob can stay over here on Thursday night. It'll be nicer for everyone. I know it's a rather mature suggestion, but I don't want to sit around here listening to you guys for hours."

"Good idea!" agreed Brian.

Mary spent the next few evenings working on her cross-country skis. The weather was changing which meant that the snow conditions were also evolving from light and powdery to heavy and sticky. She needed to remove the current wax on the bottom of her skis and replace it with one that would work under the new conditions. This was an important procedure and took several hours to complete properly. She needed to remove the old wax with a blow torch and rag, smooth the surface of each ski and then apply the new waxes and melt them onto the surface. Although there are certain waxes used for various snow types, each skier develops their own wax recipes that they believe work best. If the wax combination is not correct, a skier will expend three times the energy trying to build up momentum on the trail. A good wax base can create skis that fly over the snow, while the wrong wax will create so much friction that every stride becomes a struggle. Mary was determined to have a successful first spring run, so she took the waxing task very seriously.

While Mary hovered over her skis, Brian read. He was halfway through an epic new novel entitled *Shogun*. The story was consuming all his free time. He even took it to work to read during his breaks. This was the first saga he had read set in Asia, and he was fascinated with the historical information and descriptions of Japan during the Edo period. Between readings, he managed to find the time to set up the card table and prepare it for the Thursday night card game.

He arrived home Thursday evening loaded down with beer, junk food and rolls of coins. Mary was already home and had packed a small bag for her sleepover with Sandra. When Brian asked about her plans, Mary said that they were going to eat at the hotel and then have a few drinks in the bar and write some letters. Mary enjoyed writing letters and she had a beautiful leather zip case in which she kept her fountain pen, writing paper, stamps and special letters from friends and family. It was a ritual that Brian admired, yet he could never quite manage to sit down and put pen to paper himself.

Mary collected her things and kissed him good bye. Brian opened a beer and sat down to await the clutch of friends who would soon descend on the table. It was not long before there was a knock on the door. Brian opened it to find Eddie and Father O'Reilly kicking the snow off their boots. Eddie was wearing his infamous poker hat. It was a ridiculous cap that held a can of beer in the front. A plastic tube ran in a complicated swirling fashion from the can to Eddie's mouth. He never drank from it for the entire night, but it had become a tradition to begin the first game with a beer positioned in the cap. Father had on his lucky sweater. It was a green fisherman knit pullover with felt shamrocks sewn all over it. They looked ludicrous and it warmed Brian's heart.

Jackson, Jim and Bob arrived a few minutes later. They settled down at the table with the usual bantering and quips. Bob had some news but he was saving it for later. It was too good to just spring on the group immediately. He wanted everyone settled and content before he began to stir the pot.

Brian and Mary had brought back a garish Hawaiian sports shirt covered in palm trees and parrots for each of their friends. Brian gave each man a shirt upon arrival. Jackson had donned the lime green and pink shirt immediately. Between the beer cap, the shamrock sweater and the tropical shirt, it was beginning to look like a costume party.

Jim pulled out the cigars. Jim was actually the only one who smoked cigars, but for some reason, probably rooted in ancient Celtic male ritual, the men believed that cigars were a prerequisite for any form of male bonding. So the game began, with Pedley choking on his first cigar, Father O'Reilly singing an Irish shanty and Eddie sipping beer from his cap. "Another evening in paradise," thought Brian, as he dealt the first hand.

They were well into the evening when Bob decided to have some fun and slowly work his news into the conversation. He had purposely sipped on his beer so he would remain sober and be able to fully appreciate the inevitable reaction that would follow.

"I wonder if the girls are having as much fun as we are," he commented as Father O'Reilly dealt the cards.

"Of course they are, in their own boring sort of way," answered Brian.

"The pub is usually quite lively on a Thursday night," Father pointed out.

"True, but tonight will be quiet with all of us here," noted Brian.

"Oh I think not," said Bob, "As I was leaving to come over here it was filling up quite nicely."

"Good! You can make money in one place, while you lose money in another," chuckled Jim.

"It should be a good night," continued Bob, "although I doubt if there'll be any green Chartreuse to boost the profits."

"Very funny!" said Brian. "I won't be touching that stuff for awhile."

"I wasn't thinking of you. I was wondering if the miners would be into it again," Bob smiled as he raised an eyebrow and glanced at Brian out of the corner of his eye.

Brian did not take the bait immediately. He was in small talk mode and had not realized what Bob was insinuating. Bob patiently waited for Brian to process his comment about the miners. It actually took one more question from Brian for him to comprehend the situation.

"Why would you be wondering about the miners? What does it matter what they are drinking in their fancy bar on the compound?"

Bob tried to sound as casual as possible as he dropped the bomb, "Because they're back in town and enjoying themselves in *my* bar."

The card game continued as did the conversation around the table. It was only Brian who was silent. He continued to play and bid, but it was clear to Bob that he was digesting the news. "He's keeping his composure very well." thought Bob. "I wonder if he'll let it pass. I doubt it. The territorial instinct should be kicking in pretty soon. It was classic timing, the miners returning to town on the one night that Mary was in the bar alone and Brian was trapped in a poker game across town. How will his warped little mind deal with this gargantuan problem? Don't disappoint me Brian," thought Bob. "Let your creative juices flow. I need another good story for Nevada."

Brian showed no signs of distress, but Bob knew that his brain was working overtime. Brian had managed to turn the flaming face incident into a personal success and he had never once referred to the miners publicly as any sort of threat or menace. If he did so now, then his friends would all see him degenerate into a jealous, insecure boyfriend. This would be unacceptable for Brian. On the other hand, he could not leave Mary in treacherous territory, alone with the green plaid man. He had to think this situation through, calmly and rationally. The enemy had returned. His innocent woman was vulnerable and unprotected. My God, he suddenly realized she wasn't even sleeping at home tonight!

Chapter Thirty-One

*B*rian's head was reeling. He couldn't concentrate on the poker game. His mind was across town in the hotel pub. He had visions of Mary sitting beside green plaid man and smiling flirtatiously. He pictured the mining town doctor winking at his buddies and putting his arm around Mary. Something had to be done. He had to get over to the hotel and mark his territory. What if Mary succumbed to the advances of the handsome, young doctor?

Bob sat across the table grinning. In some ways he missed the early years of a relationship when everything is so tenuous and complicated by hormones. On the other hand, he was pleased that he didn't have to worry about Sandra. Their lives were so entwined now with dreams and finances that she would not consider opting for an alternative partner. He felt confident and secure. He had forgotten about God's sense of humour!

Brian folded his cards and stood up. He walked around the room while the others finished the hand. He was trying to devise an excuse to go over to the hotel. He needed a reason that would require everyone to join him. He could not enter the war zone without his own troops. It was Jackson who innocently opened the door when he commented that if there were visitors in town he should probably take a run around town and check in at the hotel.

"I wouldn't want to find out that there were any problems in town while I was sitting around here playing poker."

"Good idea!" piped in Brian. "We should all go with you."

The only one not thrilled with the suggestion was Eddie. He had been winning all evening and wanted to continue accumulating new wealth. They were not playing for high stakes and so, as soon as Brian offered to buy all Eddie's drinks at the hotel, he was out of his chair and throwing on his parka. Eddie grabbed everyone's keys and went out to warm up all the trucks.

"Be careful out there," he warned when he came back in the house, "It's icy as hell."

Everyone else took their turn in the bathroom and finished up their last drinks. Pedley left to cruise around town on patrol and agreed to meet up with the others at the hotel when he finished. Brian was first out of the driveway and led the small caravan of vehicles off to the bar.

Eddie was right, the weather had been mild all day, but had cooled off towards evening and the roads were covered in a smooth, thick sheet of ice. No one was too concerned. There were no other vehicles about. Brian was looking in his rear view mirror and smoothing his hair as he came to the only intersection in town. He wanted to look good when he entered the bar. Jackson had circled the neighbourhood and was cruising up to the same intersection from the opposite direction. He was looking out the passenger's window at Eddie's garage. By the time Brian and Jackson looked out their front windows again, they were heading straight at each other. Although they each tried quick manoeuvres, there was nothing much that could be done on the glare ice. The vehicles glided into each other head on. The trucks behind Brian were taken off guard. Eddie slid into Brian. Father O'Reilly tried to swerve. He missed Eddie's rear but spun around and hit the side of Brian's cab. Jim rear-ended Eddie and Bob missed all the vehicles by turning swiftly into the ditch.

For a moment everyone just sat in their cabs digesting the chain of events. When they did begin to emerge from their vehicles, it was a struggle to walk on the slippery road. They finally met up at Pedley's police truck. The first concern was for each other. Fortunately no one was hurt. They had all been driving very slowly. Once they were sure that everyone was fine, they all turned to look at the tangled mess of metal filling the intersection.

Jackson stood with his hands on his hips, shaking his head. "Well isn't this a goddamn mess! The only six vehicles on the road manage to hit each other! How the hell am I going to explain this in a report?"

"Well you don't have to write up my truck," Bob consoled, "I only drove into the ditch."

"Thanks! That makes me feel much better. It's only a five-truck pile up!"

"What the hell were you doing?" he shouted at Brian.

"What are you screaming at me for? You drove into my truck!"

The two men started throwing the blame back and forth at each other until Bob stepped in. "Look you two it seems to me it was everyone's fault. None of us should have been out here driving."

"Then what do we do?" asked Pedley.

"We blame the ice!" replied Bob.

"You're absolutely right!" injected Father O'Reilly. "These are the iciest roads I have ever seen."

"Worst conditions in thirty years!" added Jim.

"I've never seen roads this slippery!" said Eddie.

This willingness to blame the weather rather than each other diffused the panic.

"I'll call my men and tell them to tow everything back to the garage. Let's get over to the hotel so I can phone them," Eddie directed.

So the six friends slid along the treacherous road and across the hotel parking lot. On the hotel porch they turned around to take one last look at their trucks sitting together in the middle of the intersection.

"I can't believe we just did that! I've never had an accident with all my friends before," smiled Eddie.

"Another first!" laughed Brian. He had almost forgotten why they were all outside in the first place. He suddenly remembered the threat lurking inside the hotel. "My God!" he thought, "I have to get inside and save Mary!"

The men entered the bar rather timidly. They were embarrassed about the pile up and were hoping that no one had seen the slow motion collisions. To their relief, the bar was almost empty. They stood along the bar to order their first drinks. Brian asked the barmaid if Mary and Sandra had been in earlier.

"They're still here," answered the girl as she nodded to the far corner of the lounge.

Brian was leaning on the bar as he looked over his shoulder in the direction the waitress had motioned. It was not what he had expected. He elbowed Bob who was standing beside him. Bob turned to look and let out a small gasp. There in the corner sat Mary at one table and Sandra at another. Mary was sitting beside green plaid man and they were both writing intently on separate pieces of paper. Sandra was sitting with another man playing a game of chess. The four of them were so intent on their pursuits that they had not even noticed anyone entering the bar.

Brian was not sure how to react. He had been quite prepared to strut like a rooster and spar with any predators on a primal male level, but it would look foolish to behave so flamboyantly in a quiet bar. On one level, the scene was innocent enough. A game of chess and some letter writing hardly warranted intrusive measures. On the other hand, it was almost too intimate. Brian could not put his feelings into words. There was a heavy weight in the pit of his stomach. He felt as if he had missed the entire battle and lost the war.

"What do we do?" he asked Bob.

"I don't know. These guys have taken this to a whole new level. This is unknown territory for me. If we start pissing in every corner of the room, we'll look like Neanderthals!"

"They're good. They're really good! They've moved in like cats rather than wolves," sneered Brian.

"The Assyrian came down like the wolf on the fold,

And his cohorts were gleaming in silver and gold," recited Bob.

"What's that?" asked Brian.

"Some poem I had to memorize in elementary school," answered Bob.

Well we could have dealt with the *Assyrian*!" continued Brian, "But I think this is more like:

At midnight in the alley, A Tom-cat comes to wail, And he looks 'round at the women, As he swings his snaky tail."

"I don't think that's how it goes," laughed Bob.

"Well it works for me right now. What the hell are we gonna do?"

"I think the situation calls for sensitivity and trust," calculated Bob. "We have to come across as confident, intelligent and open-minded partners."

"That's gonna be tough," grimaced Brian.

"I know. You're gonna have trouble faking intelligence!"

Brian punched Bob on the shoulder and turned around to take another look at Mary.

"She's never asked me to sit down and write letters with her," complained Brian.

"That's the thing with women. They don't want to have to ask. They want you to offer. I should have offered to play chess with Sandra years ago. Once she started nagging me about the game, I knew we were in trouble. It's my fault! I bet those guys suggested that they join them. That's the move that will sweep a woman off her feet. Anyway, we shouldn't go over too soon. Right now they're in the position of power. We need to look nonchalant."

The two of them fell silent and looked down at their beers. It was Eddie who broke the silence by commenting that Brian and Bob looked like they were in mourning. He thought they were worried about their trucks and began to assure them that his men would fix up the vehicles within a day or two. Jackson had decided that he did not need to file any accident reports if the damage was minimal and no one needed to submit insurance claims. Everyone agreed that they could turn the ridiculous fender bender into a non-incident.

Brian was still trying to casually catch Mary's eye, when Bob suggested that maybe the best approach was no approach at all. When Brian looked puzzled, Bob continued to explain that by ignoring the situation it would become an insignificant event.

"We don't want to make a mountain out of a molehill," Bob cautioned. "We want to appear as men of the world; the kind of men who certainly don't mind if their women partake in quiet, intellectual pursuits with male friends."

"With effeminate friends!" smirked Brian.

"Whatever! You'd better take Mary home tonight and talk. Women like to talk. We need to counterbalance this evening with sincere, sensitive concern about their feelings and thoughts. Can you do that or do you need some tips?"

"I've got to ask lots of questions, right? How she feels when she writes the letters, that kind of thing."

"Yea! And make sure you tell her some dark, secret feeling you have."

"Like what? I don't have any dark, secret feelings."

"Make something up! They really like it if you show some vulnerability. I don't know . . . something like it frightens you to put pen to paper. You're afraid of what you may write."

"That's queer!" snorted Brian.

"Exactly!" nodded Bob.

VI

A Battle with Demons

Chapter Thirty-Two

Brian had no time for male bonding. The entire weekend was spent with Mary. He stuck so closely to her that she literally bumped into him on several occasions. On Saturday morning he went with her to the school to help her decorate a bulletin board. Saturday afternoon they went for a drive. Saturday evening they opened a bottle of wine and talked until well after midnight. Sunday morning they slept late and then Brian made breakfast. By Sunday afternoon Mary was sick of him.

Not only was Brian trying to emphasize his attractiveness and value to Mary, but he was also trying to keep her away from the hotel until green plaid man had departed town. A weekend that did not include the hotel was completely out of character for Brian. Mary was mystified. Brian was exhausted.

Late Sunday afternoon Bob and Sandra called. They wondered if Brian and Mary would like to meet them at the hotel for a drink. Mary had answered the phone and accepted the invitation before Brian could object. Mary was putting on her parka while Brian was still sitting at the kitchen table.

"What's the matter with you?" she asked. "You're not yourself this weekend."

"I don't know. I thought we could just sit and talk again tonight."

"My God! We've been talking for forty-eight hours straight! I know every experience you've had since kindergarten."

"What's wrong with that?" asked Brian.

"Nothing, Babe. I would just like to get out with our friends. It's what we do. You should understand that. How can I be a special pebble, if no one is around to feel the ripples?"

Brian laughed. "You've got a point!"

He put on his jacket and they drove to the hotel. Brian was nervous when they entered the bar. Much to his relief, no enemy troops were present. Bob and Sandra were sitting in the far corner with Father O'Reilly.

Mary went off to the washroom with Sandra, and Brian joined the table. He and Bob were comparing their weekends and telling Father O'Reilly about the Friday night crisis.

"Well you know what they say in Dublin?" chuckled the priest.

"What's that Father?" asked Bob.

"A good run is better than a bad stand!"

It felt good to be out with friends again. Mary was right. Life without friends was pretty damn dull. Brian's smile began to fade as he dwelled on the thought. Life without friends would be a travesty. How could people consider leaving good friends? He understood leaving family. He left his home without a second thought. There was no laughter in that house. He had seriously thought they would all be in Everet forever. He never imagined that these comrades would decide to move on. How could they leave him?

"Hey, are you with us?" Bob asked as he nudged Brian in the ribs. Brian glanced at his friend. He threw his arm around Bob and gave him a huge kiss on the cheek, while he rumpled his hair with the other hand. Everyone shook their heads and grinned.

"How can you think about leaving this?" grinned Brian as he spread his arms.

"You mean, how dare he think about leaving you!" smirked Mary.

"Same thing," said Brian.

The conversation shifted to the menu and what everyone was going to order. Brian was not hungry. He was annoyed at all of them. No one seemed to grasp the seriousness of the situation. It was monumental. These friends were his soul mates. They gave his life meaning. More importantly, they gave his life purpose and joy. He needed to come to terms with the impending break up.

Brian spent the rest of the evening in silence. Jackson, Jim and Eddie had come in midway through the meal. Jackson had brought a small travel book about the northwest coast. Everyone was looking through it and chatting about fjords, fish and mountain ranges. Father O'Reilly ran home to get some photos of the eastern Arctic that his future congregation had sent him. Mary asked Bob if they had any photos of Nevada and the hotel they hoped to buy. Bob went off to his office to find them.

The stimulating conversation and enthusiasm drowned out Brian's silence. They were all so excited for each other. Mary was already talking about the visits she could plan to see misty coastlines, frozen tundra and desert sage. There were open invitations offered all round. Bob was describing the Hoover Dam. Jackson was enticing everyone with the size of the king salmon at his new posting. Father was showing photos of seals and narwhal tusks. Spring was coming, and with it, new beginnings.

Brian was the only one who saw it as the end of an era. His perception was linear. Everyone around him was wrapped in a circle of friends, a circle of conversation and a circle of continuous experience. He was standing on a straight, flat path looking at a precipice. He could see no forks in the road.

He had been so consumed by this place and these friendships that he had closed all doors leading to other places. All his energy had been expended on making this place perfect. As he looked around the table it suddenly struck him that everyone there had a vocation; a teacher, a police officer, a priest, an innkeeper, a mechanic and a gas fitter. These people could move on. They had expertise that every community needed. No wonder Mary had looked at the doctor.

Brian had not looked in the mirror for a long time; the mirror that reflects the essence of a person. "Who am I?" he wondered. This inner voyage depressed him even more than his earlier thoughts. It would become all consuming over the next few weeks. The dark side of Brian was about to re-emerge. He was a man of extremes. In a matter of days he had moved from outrageous and comical, to morose and self-indulgent. He would begin to fight old demons again. Demons that he thought had been slaughtered and buried. He was too young to realize that demons can never be cut and quartered. That's the nature of a demon. They return at the most unexpected of times.

Mild depression can be easily recognized. It sends out numerous signals. Victims may stop bathing and caring for themselves. They may drink alcohol to excess and never leave the house. They escape into long periods of sleep. They rarely smile. Friends and family can hear the cry for help. Good friends and family will listen.

Serious depression is more obtuse. It kidnaps the victim without any signal to the outside world. Except for a light ringing in the ears, there are no physical signs. People faithfully go through the motions of each day. They continue to function on one level, even though they have been mentally removed to another place. The black hole envelops them. It is almost a form of astral travel. Victims feel disconnected from their bodies. The irony is that there is not much conscious thought, so they watch dispassionately. They have no interest in the person they have left behind. They sleep very little. They think even less. If the demon is put back in the black box from which it came, they will not remember much of the visit. The mind is a powerful friend. In its attempts to survive the demon, it shuts down and denies the monster access to its memory bank.

Brian was on such a voyage. Unfortunately no one knew he was away.

Chapter Thirty-Three

It was a glorious spring. The sun shone almost every day. When it did snow, it was in huge, luscious flakes that floated rather than fell to the ground. It created scenes that the world loves to romanticize on Christmas cards and in old movies.

Mary skied every weekend. The men spent their time ice fishing on a nearby lake. It had been a cold and windy winter. Without much snow cover on the lake, the ice was thicker than usual. They had worked hard to cut the hole. Jim had to bring out his biggest chainsaw. The ice measured more than two feet in thickness. It meant they would be able to fish well into May before it was too thin to tread upon.

Eddie had found the spot. His friends had given him the task and he had taken the duty seriously. Usually they chose a spot just off the road, so they could drive the trucks onto the lake.

This year, Eddie had explored on snowmobile. It meant another hour in travel time, but everyone was pleased when they arrived at the area Eddie had marked out in March. It was isolated and private. It was located on a deep inlet, so there was a magnificent view of trees on three sides of the hole. The evergreens were covered in a foot of April snow and their branches hung heavy toward the ground. The place was conducive to quiet thought and contemplation.

Jackson had brought out his large tent and wood stove. Bob supplied all the cooking paraphernalia. Jim had stored their chairs and benches over the winter. Father O'Reilly and Eddie purchased the food supplies. Brian brought the beer. Although they each had long, Arctic sleds attached to their snowmobiles, Bob and Jim had to return to the trucks for a second load. Once they were initially settled, further visits to the site would be simple. The only thing they had to bring back each time was the food. Food would attract animals, and animals could destroy a camp. They would leave the other supplies at the hole until the spring breakup when the ice would be in final meltdown.

Brian had also brought two large rocks on his sled. As they set up camp, he placed them at the hole, between two of the chairs.

"What the hell are those for?" asked Bob.

"They're special pebbles," answered Brian.

"They're not pebbles, they're fuckin' boulders!" laughed Jim.

"Well, just think of them as new friends," Brian said. "I thought we could sit on them."

"I suspect they're smarter than half of us," smiled Father O'Reilly, "but if you sit on them you're gonna get haemorrhoids for sure!"

"Nothin' funny about piles," injected Jackson, "they hurt like hell."

It took about an hour to set up the camp. They pitched Jackson's huge tent over the hole, lit the wood stove and put a pot of water on top to boil. By the time they were ready to sit down in a circle around the hole and drop in their fishing lines, the place was warm and cosy. In a few weeks when the weather warmed, they would move the tent off to the side of the hole. At the moment it was still too cold.

The group had been setting up spring ice fishing camp for a few years now and they travelled in relative luxury. They had six cots that sat a foot off the ground. They placed them around the perimeter of the tent. Bob even brought along his portable Johnny, so no one had to freeze outside in the middle of the night. There were several jokes made about Eddie and the portable loo. Father O'Reilly and Jim had brought along room spray. They said that Eddie's morning constitutional had almost killed them the previous year.

They caught several nice rainbow trout on the first afternoon. Jackson and Eddie rode over to the far shore of the lake to gut and fillet the fish. This way the remains would be left to animals in the vicinity without drawing them over to the tent area. They returned to the smell of frying potatoes and corn on the cob roasting in the woodstove. A large sheet of thick plywood had been placed over the ice hole and the camp table positioned above it. They sat down to a feast.

The food was delicious, the conversation rich and warm. They talked about every crazy thing they had done in the past few years; Johnny Michael's wake, the curling stone vendetta and the body snatching. Jim noted that they had calmed down since the kidnapping. They all agreed the event had twisted back on them and halted any further urges to play practical jokes. Bob reminded them that Brian had continued the tradition by leaping off the balcony in Maui.

"Yes, but that was me, not us," Brian noted.

"I guess we're getting dull in our old age," smiled Father O'Reilly.

"And moving on," added Brian.

Pragmatic meanings can sometimes fall on deaf ears. Brian's intention was to utter a sad, concluding statement. It was accepted by the group as a positive introduction to a new conversation. They began to chat enthusiastically about Jackson and Father O'Reilly's transfers. Bob announced that they had just received a good offer on the hotel. Eddie and Jim began talking about wintering in Nevada.

At one point in the evening, Eddie had gone behind the makeshift curtain to sit on the portable commode. Shortly thereafter everyone flayed with dramatic gestures and groans as they raced from the tent to escape the odour. As they emerged from their den, the joking stopped abruptly. They stood in awe.

The night sky was gone. A vibrant blanket of multi-coloured waves hung over the lake. It was late in the season for such spectacular northern lights. The men had seen aurora borealis many times. Most often they were greenish waves covering half to a third of the sky near the horizon. These lights were different. Green, blue and even red waves filled the entire sky.

"Can you hear it?" whispered Father O'Reilly.

Everyone nodded. They were privy to the mysterious crackling sound that trappers often recount. Scientists have yet to record the sound, but too many witnesses have described it to deny its existence. They each lay down on the seats of their snowmobiles to enjoy the spectacle. It was truly amazing. After about twenty minutes Bob broke the silence.

"I won't see these in Nevada."

"True, but you also won't be freezing your ass off! I'm going back inside." Jim pulled his fur hat over his ears.

"Is it safe to come back in?" Jackson hollered from his snowmobile.

"Yea, the smell is gone," yelled Jim from the tent.

"Very funny," Eddie muttered.

They warmed up, loaded the stove with wood and crawled into their cots. The banter degenerated into comments about snoring and farting. Everyone warned Eddie not to use the toilet during the night. The conversation slowly dwindled and it was not long before everyone was sleeping soundly, everyone that is except Brian. He slipped out of the tent again and lay down on a snow machine to look at the sky once more. He was numb. "Take me. Please just take me." If God heard, he did not take action. He rarely does when we ask to be released of our duties prematurely. The night continued and at some point Brian returned to the tent and his cot.

They awoke to a clear morning. After coffee, they all donned their sunglasses to go outside. The combination of sun and snow was blinding. Jim, Bob and Eddie rode off on their snowmobiles to explore. Jackson and Father O'Reilly trekked across the lake on snowshoes and disappeared into the forest. Brian went back inside the tent and sat on one of the rocks. It is difficult to ascertain what musings exist during a depression, since our memories fail us later. He appeared to be deep in thought, although if someone were to have offered him a penny, he would not have been able to accept it. Time had no meaning. When the others returned, Brian did not know if they had been gone for a few minutes or a few hours.

They had hooked their rods up and dropped their lines in the hole before leaving. Jim started lunch while Bob took the fish to the far shore for cleaning. After they ate it was time to pack up. It would take a couple of hours to reach town. They placed the remaining food in the storage space under the snowmobile seats. The Arctic sleds were left at the camp. This made the return trip faster and much more fun. They could manoeuvre the machines over embankments, swerve and glide around trees and jump small ridges.

Father O'Reilly had a winter trademark. He wore a bright green scarf knotted and wrapped around his neck with a long portion of it hanging down the front of his parka. In the north, scarves are wrapped around the neck first and then the parka is put on over the scarf. It is too cold to use a scarf as a decorative accessory. This habit of the Irish priest was a left over fashion statement from the old country. During his first winter in Everet, he soon realized the importance of the inner scarf. He had bought a second one and continued to wrap the green muffler on the outside, in the usual manner.

The men were racing across a wide expanse. They were all standing up on their machines to balance themselves over the rough terrain. Suddenly Father O'Reilly began to lean forward and slow down. It took a few minutes for the others to realize that he was no longer beside them. They circled and returned to his machine which had stopped. When they arrived at his side, the priest was kneeling on the seat of his snowmobile with his head resting on the handlebars.

"What's the matter Father?" shouted Bob.

"I can't breathe," croaked the priest.

Everyone jumped off their machines and ran to his side. Somehow, Father's ridiculous green scarf had entangled itself in the snowmobile engine. The mechanisms had pulled the muffler further and further into the front of the machine. The scarf had tightened around O'Reilly's neck and started to choke him. His classic knot was so tight that there was no hope of loosening it. He was in real pain. Jim took out his hunting knife and carefully cut the scarf off. Once it was established that the priest was okay, the jokes began.

"Finally! The death of the green boa!" bellowed Jackson.

"Father we love you, but I can't say we're sorry to see that stupid scarf gone," said Bob affectionately.

The priest was still rubbing his neck and turning his head from side to side.

"I'm not going to disagree with you. Right now I hate the damn thing!"

Eddie worked on the engine to disentangle the remains of the woollen appendage. Everyone agreed that it was lucky to have happened when others were around.

"Imagine if you had been alone," said Bob. "It was cinched damned tight. You could have starved to death out here."

"Everyone would have thought it was some kind of weird suicide," laughed Jackson.

"Priest chooses green wool over rope!" added Eddie as he pulled the last of the dead scarf from the engine and held it high.

"Come on! Let's get back to town before the sun sets," said Bob.

"And if the roads are icy, I want to see a mile between each truck!" yelled Jackson.

Chapter Thirty-Four

Sunday morning, Brian was awoken by a thousand voices. It sounded like a huge cocktail party. He rolled onto his back and listened. It was amazing. He tried to catch snippets of one or two conversations. He could not. He tried to identify the music playing in the background. He could not. But he recognized the melody. He had been to this gathering before.

Mary and Brian's house stood beside open marshland. Each spring, migrating swans would stop to rest on their way back to the Arctic coast. Thousands of white birds would descend on the wetlands. Once they were all grounded, their banter sounded exactly like a huge cocktail party.

The first time they had heard the return of the swans, Mary and Brian had jumped out of bed to investigate the commotion. They were sure the entire town was in their driveway. It had been a haunting experience.

Mary had been surprised that wild swans existed. She had only seen the lovely tame ones floating on lakes and streams. The only difference between the two is the colour of the beak. The Mute swan that glides along the Avon has an orange beak, other species have black beaks.

They fly in formation like all wild geese. To watch thousands take flight and glide into a wedge formation is a privilege. Brian felt a sudden urgent need to witness the miracle. He dressed quietly and left the house. It was a short walk to the edge of the marsh. He made himself comfortable on a large snow bank. It would be awhile before the enormous gaggle decided to depart.

The chatter of the geese flowed through Brian. It was comforting. The sounds blended perfectly with the voices already in his head. He had been consumed by murmurings for weeks; a multitude of whispers with no clear message. It felt good to hear the same hum outside his body. He lay back on the snow and closed his eyes.

He was enveloped in soothing vibrations. It was reassuring. He had blended into the world around him. No annoying interruptions from his own disturbing hauntings. This could not be called blissful. Brian was not enjoying the moment. But for a few moments he was released from his perceived doom of the real world. Somewhere in the black hole, the demons were lost in the clamber of the geese. "Take me." He pleaded. Then it happened. The chatter ended and the birds rose in a wave. They magically fell into formation, first several chevrons, then gliding into one massive skein. Silence descended. Brian watched them until they were a small black dot on the horizon. They were gone. He was empty. The silence pounded on his temples.

Brian lay for another hour on the snow bank before returning to the house. Mary was up and sipping her first cup of tea when he entered the kitchen. He poured a coffee and sat down beside her.

"Were they wonderful?"

"Mmmm, until they left."

"Aren't things still wonderful after they leave?"

"I don't know. You tell me."

Mary could not bear Brian's recent mood. She found it self-indulgent. Rather than sharing anticipation with his friends, he was totally absorbed with himself. She was witness to a side of Brian she did not like. "His was a selfish love," she thought. "He thinks he loves his friends to excess, but he's consumed with his pending loss. How selfish is that?"

Mary was bearing the brunt of Brian's change in mood. Since the return from Hawaii, he had become more distant. There was less conversation, less laughter and less intimacy. Their friends' new prospects had excited Mary. The more they spoke of their moves, the more interested she had become in doing something new and exciting. She had tossed a few ideas past Brian. Her sister lived in Bombay, they could go there. He thought the idea was stupid. They both had Celtic roots, what about Scotland? He was not interested. Bermuda accepted Canadian teachers and there would be no more winter. He would feel trapped on an island.

"He's not interested in me anymore," she thought. She had always thought that if they parted, it would be in a civilized manner. She was annoyed with his attitude. She interpreted his responses as signals. He could not have an honest conversation about his changing feelings, so it was easier to drive her away with negativity. She began to imagine life without Brian.

"Sandra called," said Mary, "We're going to meet at noon. We thought it would be nice to ride out to the hot springs for the afternoon. Everyone is coming. Would you care to join us?"

"Why not," Brian answered.

Most hot springs around the world are ancient social sites. The human need to control ensures that massive buildings stand over the springs. Pools have been built to capture the healing waters. People no longer see the magic force bubbling from the ground. The smell of sulphur is the only remaining link to nature.

The Everet Springs sat undisturbed by human design. They nestled against a hill on the edge of a mountain valley. The steaming water gushed into an upper pool. It cascaded over rocks into the middle pool. Then it travelled underground to the lower pool. It was very hot. The upper pool was more than one hundred and ten degrees.

The temperatures dropped as the mineral water flowed into the lower pools. Each pool had been carved in stone by a millennium of hot, rippling water, the ledges and floor worn smooth to silky perfection.

The springs were a local secret. They were a one hour ride by snowmobile. When the group arrived and the machines shut down, everyone stood for a moment in silent tribute. The steam rising from the waters surrounded by pristine clouds of snow was stunning.

"Ahhh, to know beauty one must live with it," murmured Father O'Reilly.

They quickly stripped down to their bathing suits and slid into the pools. Everyone chose the middle pool except Brian who slid into the extreme uppermost pond.

"There must be a better description of this place than beautiful," said Bob.

"Magnificent," offered Eddie.

"Resplendent," smiled Mary.

"Pulchritudinous," said Jackson thoughtfully nodding his head.

"What kind of goddamn word is that?" laughed Bob, "It sounds like a disease!"

"Pedley, you never cease to amaze me," chuckled Father O'Reilly, shaking his head.

"I'm not just another pretty face with a gun," answered Jackson, raising an eyebrow and lowering his lids.

"Don't remind me. It terrifies me every time I think of you armed," said Jim.

"I'd like to remind you that I'm the defender of this great nation!"

In days of yore, from Britain's shore,
Wolfe the dauntless hero came,
And planted firm Britannia's flag,

On Canada's fair domain," sang Jim as he rose and placed his right hand over his heart.

The others rose and joined in, "Here may it wave, our boast, our pride, And joined in love together, The thistle, shamrock, rose entwine, The Maple Leaf forever!"

"My God, I haven't sung that since Kindergarten," laughed Mary.

"Can't sing it anymore," said Bob "Upsets the French!"

"Don't get me started on The Plains of Abraham!" grumbled Jim, "How many times have we fought that battle since 1759?"

"*The Two Solitudes*, the Canadian dilemma," added Bob.

"Have you read that book, Pedley?" asked Jim.

"Of course I've read MacLennan!" answered Jackson, "That's where I first read pulchritudinous."

"Sure you did!" continued Bob, "It's a beautiful thing, the French-English love affair in this country."

"That's enough politics! It upsets my stomach," said Jim.

Brian sat silently while he stared down at the lower pools. No one noticed his isolation except Mary. She was staring at him when she noticed movement behind his head. There perched on a tall spruce tree was her white owl. As she gazed up at him, she suddenly remembered her grandmother telling her that owls always came to console individuals through times of trouble. "Are you here to comfort me my friend?" As the question floated in her mind, the owl turned its head and looked directly down at Brian.

The conversation subsided as everyone slid further into the soothing waters. They alternated between soaking in the springs and rolling in the colossal snow mounds. They made snow angels. They pitched snowballs at one another. Eddie even had a nap on a snow bank. The glorious sunshine, the sparkling snow and the healing waters created an icy Eden. Life was good.

Chapter Thirty-Five

The snowmobiles pulled up to the Everet Hotel. The group dismounted slowly. The hot springs had taken their toll. Everyone was tired. They drifted into the inn for dinner. Bob announced that he had ordered in a special meal. He left everyone in the lobby and went into the hotel kitchen. When he returned he had the group follow him to Room 102. They entered the room and trailed behind him into the small bathroom. There in the tub were eight huge lobsters.

"Direct from the east coast!" Bob announced. "They came in on the flight this afternoon."

"They're magnificent!" grinned Jim.

"A special meal, for a special group," smiled Sandra.

"On a very special day!" pronounced Bob.

When they returned to the restaurant Bob directed them to a small enclave off the main dining room. The staff had prepared a lovely table and the chef was overseeing the settings.

"It's gorgeous!" gasped Mary.

"It's not often I get to prepare a real meal in this sorry place," spouted the chef.

Bob clipped him affectionately on the back of the head as they all sat down to feast. Three bottles of Dom Perignon 1975 champagne were delivered to the table. The staff opened them with much fanfare. Then Bob rose to toast the gathering.

"Don't worry about the future, The present is all thou hast, The future will soon be present, And the present will soon be past . . . to friends!"

Everyone clinked glasses and sipped the superb wine. Father rose to add his Irish wisdom, "May you have the hindsight to know where you've been, the foresight to know where you are going, and the insight to know when you've gone too far."

They toasted again, as Eddie grimaced, "Mmmm, Johnny Michael."

"Yea, we went a little too far with that one," grinned Jim.

"I think you each paid the price. The guilt almost killed you," smiled Father.

Mary leaned over to Sandra and asked her what had prompted such a celebration. Sandra explained that the hotel sale had been finalized and the money transferred. She and Bob would be leaving in six weeks for sunny Nevada. The two friends hugged each other long and hard.

Jim had overheard the women. "It's a done deal! You're off to the sunny south!"

Bob smiled and nodded. There were handshakes and back patting all around. Brian stared at his friends. "The future will soon be present," he thought as he slowly twirled his wine glass.

"I've got some news too!" boasted Jim, "The wife and I are heading out in June."

"Where to?" asked Pedley.

"We want real isolation. Someplace where we can get lost and spend the rest of our lives in quiet solitude. We've worn out the atlas over the past few years, but we've finally decided on a place."

"And where would that be?" asked Father O'Reilly.

"The Falkland Islands!"

"The what?" asked Pedley.

"The Falkland Islands. They're in the Atlantic, off the coast of Argentina. Just a bunch of sheep farmers, mostly Scottish origins."

"I've never heard of them," said Mary.

"Exactly the point," continued Jim, "No one has. The population is about the same as up here. The capital is a small town called Stanley, about the same as Whitehorse."

"And just what exactly are you going to do on the Falklands?" asked Brian with a hint of sarcasm that only Mary noticed.

"We've bought a small hotel. The owner is also the propane supplier, so I bought his equipment as well. We'll never be rich, but we'll be comfortable. And we'll be as far away from the politics and bull shit as we can get."

"The Falkland Islands! That's obscure all right. I need to see your atlas," laughed Bob.

"Now we have a place to stay in Nevada and on the Falkland Islands," Mary smiled and looked up at the ceiling, "How will I ever decide where to vacation?"

"Tough call," chuckled Pedley.

"Even your friends don't want to visit you!" groaned Eddie.

"There's a weekly flight from Argentina," grinned Jim, "You're always welcome, when you feel the need to escape."

"Peace and tranquillity," murmured Mary.

"Scotsmen and sheep!" added Bob.

"The Scots are just Irishmen gone astray. A little more serious, a little less stubborn and a lot more frugal," said Father O'Reilly.

"Frugal for sure!" laughed Mary, "My grandfather always said that the Scots only have a sense of humour because it's free."

Time trickled into a wide meandering fraternal communion. The more alcohol they consumed, the more their expressions of mutual devotion intensified. They relived every moment of their time together in Everet. There were howls over the curling stone theft and colourful descriptions of the Japanese entourage. They mused over Mary's flight from Whitehorse with Kevin. Bob was asked more than once to describe Brian's leap from the Maui balcony. Curling bonspiels were relived and various games replayed. Johnny Michael's wake came up several times throughout the evening. Re-creations of the look on Jackson's face when he found himself frozen to Johnny's corpse and his expression when Eddie pissed on him provided endless amusement. A good portion of time was spent trying to piece together the journey of Johnny's corpse around town.

There was a moment's silence for Brad Kincaid and his family. There were no appropriate words. Each of them had experienced the pain and frustration of that long, winter night. The conversation darkened as they began to discuss life and death; nebulous speculations on manifest destiny versus a random universe. Father O'Reilly defended the master plan, while Bob played the devil's advocate.

Jackson lightened the mood by insisting that there was a Mountie paradise. Brian asked him for a detailed description. The officer could not provide one, but he was sure there would be no trips to the hospital with friends who had facial wounds from green Chartreuse. Their faces lit up. They had all forgotten about Brian's head going up in flames.

"Brian, old friend, you've given me enough material for a lifetime of storytelling!" smiled Bob as he dug into his last lobster claw.

"And I'm sure they'll improve with age," Sandra said, flicking a piece of shell at him.

"Isn't that the secret? To enhance memories as they fade," asked Bob, "Life is merely a collection of experiences, here today, gone tomorrow. It's up to us whether we choose to remember or forget. The tale spinner's duty is to bring a delicate and glorious incident back to the present, even if it's only for a moment."

"Like hoarfrost and cherry blossoms," sighed Mary, "delicate and fleeting."

"But with a huge dose of humour," added Father, "the magic ingredient is levity."

"Good Lord, yes!" Bob replied, "If you don't appreciate the bizarre, the random and the ridiculous, then you haven't begun to grasp the nature of life. It's all so goddamn funny! My God is definitely a comedian."

"What about the God of vengeance?" Mary asked.

"That was just King James' version to keep the masses working hard and paying taxes!" sneered Father O'Reilly.

"No politics, Father!" chuckled Bob.

"That's why I'm moving to the Falklands," said Jim, "No more flag-waving, no more arguments. French, English, Protestant, Catholic . . . I'm sick of it all!"

Chapter Thirty-Six

*I*t was the second Sunday in May. Father O'Reilly entered the sacristy in thoughtful reverence. It would be the last time he donned the vestments of St. Paul's Church. He was slow and methodical this morning. He took the alb from the closet and placed it carefully over his head, letting the long, white robe fall to his feet. The linen tunic was immaculate; pure white and pressed to perfection. He held the long, black cincture in both hands and then tied the silk cord around his waist.

He looked in the mirror, turning from side to side. "Well Peter O'Reilly, thank God for the chasuble," he said to himself. "You've gained weight over the past few years. This alb and cincture is not as becoming as it once was."

He opened the drawer next to the closet and removed the beautiful silk stole. He kissed the cross and placed the stole over his head so the embroidered cross was centred on the back of his neck. He adjusted the alb to ensure it sat high enough on his neck to protect the valuable stole hanging over it.

Then Father Peter O'Reilly carefully removed the heavy chasuble from the oak closet. It was magnificent. The designer must have been Irish, he thought. So many shades of green were present on the damask brocade. It reminded the priest of an aerial view of his beloved Ireland. He hesitated for a moment. He should be donning the white and gold chasuble as it was the 5th Sunday of Easter. The fine, green gown was not scheduled until the first Sunday of Pentecost which would begin on May 29th. Vanity prevailed. He wanted to wear his favourite colours on this final Sabbath in Everet. The two altar boys helped him place the heavy garment over his head. He looked in the mirror once more. He was sure that his next posting would not include such fine vestments.

The green robe was worn for ordinary Sundays. It was interesting that his favourite colour was considered 'ordinary'. It was also interesting that the most expensive vestment was the one worn most often during the year. The priest often speculated on the history of the chasuble. This was not a wealthy congregation. The church was small and the design simple. Except for the Stations of the Cross along the two side walls, and a small statue of Mary in the back corner, it could be mistaken for a protestant place of worship. This parish had embraced Pope Paul VI and ecumenicism. It suited the north to embrace differences. Often services were held here with multi-faith participants. Yet at some point in time, this stunning, traditional robe had been purchased.

Father O'Reilly had thought long and hard about his final homily. It was important. His congregation had invited the entire community to this mass as a final farewell to their popular priest. He loved the people of Everet and he wanted to leave them with a special message.

He had decided that he would keep the homily short. Since the group would be ecumenical, he would then step down from the pulpit and give a personal message to the gathering. He could refer to the Gospel reading again in his informal speech, since today it was John 13:31-35. "Most appropriate," he thought, "with its themes of comings and goings and its reference to love one another."

The church was packed when Father O'Reilly entered from the back and slowly walked down the aisle. His eyes filled with tears, as people turned to smile and nod at him; so many faces, so many memories. Bob winked at him. Mary smiled warmly. Eddie gave him a thumbs up. How would he manage to get through this mass without sobbing like a baby?

He pulled himself together and the mass proceeded smoothly. After the homily, Father O'Reilly stepped down from the pulpit and stood in front of the altar. He spent some time looking at each face smiling at him. Then he began.

"We learn the message of the Church in our first few years on earth. Then we spend a lifetime delving deeper; reading, thinking, discussing, analysing. But like all important knowledge, we find ourselves coming full circle; right back to the beginning again. It's a simple message. Jesus said it more than once. God is love. That's it! That's all you really need to know. We teach every child that message in their early church lessons. God is love. If we could only come to grips with that one concept and embrace it. Everything else would fall into place quite nicely. God is love.

He helps us at the beginning by introducing us to love through our families. But we can love our families without any help from God. He knows that. So he doesn't command us to 'love' our father and mother, does he? He tells us to honour our mother and father. God also knows all about our egos. He knows that most of us love ourselves excessively. So he tells us to love our neighbour as we love ourselves.

And that is our mandate. It may be unconscious but we spend our time on earth, trying to learn how to love. If we're lucky then each experience brings us a tiny bit closer to the perfection. This community has helped me on my personal journey. You have taught me so much about love. Love of life. Love of laughter. Love of friendship. Love of snow and freezing temperatures!" Everyone chuckled.

"The older we get, the more we realize just how delicate this thing called 'life' is. We hold on to it by a tenuous thread. It's a fleeting second. One sweet, beautiful moment in time; like hoarfrost and cherry blossoms." He winked at Mary as a thank you for using her phrase. "Keep your eyes wide open or you'll miss it. And if you're lucky enough to see it, appreciate the second in time, and love it! That's all you need to know. God is love."

He opened his arms to the congregation and smiled, "May almighty God bless you, the Father, and the Son and the Holy Spirit. Go in peace and love."

Years later, Father O'Reilly would try to remember leaving the church, but he could not. He would remember only one image, Brian's face moments later.

Chapter Thirty-Seven

Everyone was gathered outside the church. It was a wonderful, sunny May morning. There was small talk and laughter as people took their turn with Father O'Reilly, to say good-bye and wish him good luck.

Mary was enjoying herself, but she was also angry. Brian had not appeared for the service. How dare he wallow in his own self pity, rather than say good bye properly to a dear friend. She was not impressed. They would definitely be having a serious discussion later about their relationship and about life in general!

Suddenly the noise of a small aircraft halted conversation. A Cessna appeared from behind the church and buzzed the crowd. People instinctively lowered their heads as the plane whizzed past.

"That's my plane!" yelled Kevin.

As it made a wide circle, a trailing banner could be seen that read "Farewell Father". The plane returned and flew low over the group once again. This time people looked up. There, looking down from the cockpit and waving, was Brian.

"That asshole has stolen my plane! Pedley do something!" screamed Kevin.

"Sure Kevin. Let me just run and get my horse!" answered Jackson.

"He's done it again," grinned Bob.

"Done what?" asked Eddie.

"Stolen the show," replied Bob.

"What a grand finale to a wonderful few years! God love him," beamed Father O'Reilly.

"My Brian is back again," thought Mary. "He's come to terms with everything. Now we can move on. The dark days are over. My God I love that man!"

Bob put his arm around Jim and said, "I hope you find the peace and tranquillity that you're looking for on those godforsaken islands, friend. I hope you love The Falklands!"

"I love that Cessna! He'd better be careful!" Kevin was following the small plane through misty eyes.

With all this talk of love, a minor mass hysteria flowed through the gathering. Pedley grabbed Mary and they began to polka. Eddie and Father O'Reilly linked arms and circled. Everyone joined in with twirls and jigs. As Brian made his last, low flyover, his heart filled to the brim. "What a ridiculous scene! What a life! A life worth dying for!" He laughed out loud as he watched the show below. "I love a good ending!"

He was still looking back and smiling when the plane smashed into the huge TranGas propane tank. The explosion was deafening. The dancing stopped.

The next four days were a nightmare. Flames were fought. Wreckage cleared. Various hopeless attempts carried out to find remains. At the end of it all, Jackson stood beside Mary for one last, silent look at the scene.

Brian was dead. Jackson put his arm around Mary and guided her back to the truck and then drove her to the hotel. They did not speak. Jackson pulled up to the hotel and helped Mary out of the truck and guided her into a safe, warm room full of friends and conversation. Father O'Reilly held out his arms and she rested her head on his shoulder. They could hear Eddie laughing and telling the story of how they had stolen Johnny Michael out of the RCMP freezer. "My God Brian was funny!" someone said.

Mary wasn't ready for storytelling yet. She was full of anger and guilt. She looked up at Father O'Reilly, "I didn't even say good bye."

"Not many of us do Mary."

"It isn't fair!"

"Brian would tell you that life isn't about fairness. He'd tell you it's about the irony, the dark humour, the ridiculousness of it all. And he did say good bye. He said good bye in a very spectacular way! Brian has moved on. But it's not about death. It's about life; this delicate, tenuous, fleeting piece of eternity that comes and goes so swiftly. It's about this room full of friends who love you, gathered around laughing and talking about your antics, your accomplishments, and your essence. It's about friends who will miss you for the rest of their lives. It's about loving every moment and releasing the demons that will eat away at your body. It's about finding humour and joy in every event. It's about appreciating the special moments, like hoarfrost and cherry blossoms."

The End

LaVergne, TN USA
20 October 2010
201621LV00001B/6/P